The

Bookshop
by the Seaside

De-ann Black

Paperback edition published 2021

The Bookshop by the Seaside

ISBN: 9798706362584

Also by De-ann Black (Romance, Action/Thrillers & Children's books). See her Amazon Author page or website for further details about her books, screenplays, illustrations, art and fabric designs.
www.De-annBlack.com

Romance:
The Sewing Bee
The Quilting Bee
Snow Bells Wedding
Snow Bells Christmas
Summer Sewing Bee
The Chocolatier's Cottage
Christmas Cake Chateau
The Beemaster's Cottage
The Sewing Bee By The Sea
The Flower Hunter's Cottage
The Christmas Knitting Bee
The Sewing Bee & Afternoon Tea
The Tea Shop
The Vintage Sewing & Knitting Bee
Shed In The City
The Bakery By The Seaside
Champagne Chic Lemonade Money
The Christmas Chocolatier
The Christmas Tea Shop & Bakery
The Vintage Tea Dress Shop In Summer
Oops! I'm The Paparazzi
The Bitch-Proof Suit
The Tea Dress Shop At Christmas

Action/Thrillers: Love Him Forever.   Someone Worse.
Electric Shadows.   The Strife Of Riley.   Shadows Of Murder.

Children's books: Faeriefied. Secondhand Spooks. Poison-Wynd. Wormhole Wynd. Science Fashion. School For Aliens.

Colouring books:
Summer Garden. Spring Garden. Autumn Garden. Sea Dream. Festive Christmas. Christmas Garden. Flower Bee. Wild Garden. Faerie Garden Spring. Flower Hunter. Stargazer Space. Bee Garden.

Contents

CHAPTER ONE

Pressed Flower Books

Bea's two favourite scents were the sea — and bookshops.

Standing outside the bookshop that overlooked the Scottish seashore, she breathed in the fresh sea air. The morning sunlight shone through the windows, casting a warm glow across the books on display. Soon she'd step into the pretty cottage bookshop she was now the owner of in a seaside location by the harbour in the Highlands.

Waves of excitement rippled through her at the prospect of seeing inside the premises — a traditional cream–painted cottage converted into a bookshop combined with a cosy cottage she could live in.

Working from home had always appealed to her, but she'd never thought that running her own bookshop would be part of it. She'd loved browsing in bookshops ever since she was a little girl and enjoyed nothing more than the comforting atmosphere of a bookshop.

Moving from the city, leaving Glasgow behind along with her accountancy job to start afresh in the Highlands, was an adventure in itself. Investing every penny she'd saved over the past ten years into buying a bookshop in a small community beside the sea was so out of step with her cautious character. But now in her early thirties she felt the need to jolt herself out of the rut she was in that provided financial security of sorts but only tiny pockets of happiness. A substantial part of her happiness was found in the books she read after coming home from the finance firm to her flat. Although in the heart of the city, her life had very little true happiness in it. Romance had a lot to do with this, or lack of it to be precise. Failed relationships with men from the office, as this was her main source of boyfriends, two in the past four years, had pushed her further into the safe world of books. Within a book she could explore the globe, visit amazing locations, meet wonderful people, and fall in love with the heroes of the romances she had a preference for. Maybe she was looking for love in all the right places, and yet, they were fictional.

1

The real world was scary a lot of the time, and challenging, not least when she saw the advertisement for the bookshop and thought — I'd love to own a bookshop and live in a cottage by the sea.

An idyllic life enticed her to contact the estate agent, and after discussions and a virtual tour of the premises, she made a bid for the quick sale of the shop. The owner, Acair, had retired earlier than planned when the woman he'd loved for years finally agreed to marry him. But the woman lived in Dundee and didn't want to move away from her family, so having no family of his own, he'd decided to leave the bookshop and start afresh with her in Dundee.

The quick sale was a bargain, but it was hoped that the new owner would keep the cottage as a bookshop because the local community depended on it, and he loathed the idea that all those marvellous books would be discarded.

Fortunately, Bea's offer was accepted along with the assurance that she intended to continue to run the bookshop. They'd taken her at her word, a refreshing change from the numerous broken promises she'd endured for several years.

Acair owned a boat and sailed off, with his new bride, quite literally, into the sunset from the village harbour. He'd closed the bookshop door for the last time in the New Year, locked it secure, and taken a final glance at the shop that was glistening with frost and sprinkled with snowflakes.

The bookshop had remained on ice, frozen for most of the New Year, in thick frost and snow, but was now blossoming in the spring.

The postmaster and several other local residents, members of the sewing bee, had kept the online sales ticking over until a new owner was found. Orders were posted out once a week. Customers knew that the actual bookshop had closed temporarily and were eagerly waiting for it to reopen. A sign on the door stated: *Closed but opening again soon.*

Bea looked at the front window of the shop, seeing her reflection. The soft white scarf she'd knitted herself was draped around the neck of her warm grey wool coat. The glass shone in the morning sunlight and she peeked through at the array of books. Flutters of excitement filled her stomach. She couldn't wait to step inside. She'd been given instructions that the key was in the safe keeping of the owner of the local post office, the postmaster.

Pulling herself away from peering in at the books, Bea looked around her. A row of little shops faced the sea. The bookshop was near the far end of the row. The rear garden backed on to one of the fields. The front had hanging baskets that someone had tended to because spring flowers were blooming and the foliage trailed down beautifully.

Bea walked past several shops, some converted cottages like hers, and went into the post office. The postmaster was chatting to a woman. Her silvery blonde hair was pinned up in a tidy bun and she was wearing a lovely lavender cardigan. Hand knitted no doubt. Gorgeous yarn. Bea loved to knit and recognised the quality of the yarn and expertise of the knitting. It was way beyond her skill level.

The chatter stopped as the postmaster recognised the newcomer.

'Hello, there, Bea. I've got the keys to the bookshop for you right here.' He reached under the counter and produced a set of keys, dangling them with great delight.

Bea was taken aback. *He knew her?*

'The estate agent emailed a photo of you. And with that lovely red hair, I recognised you right away.'

Bea's titian hair fell in soft, silky waves to her shoulders and emphasised her pretty, pale features and inquisitive green eyes.

She went over and accepted the keys. 'Thank you.'

He turned to the woman. 'Ethel, this is Bea, the new owner of the bookshop.'

Ethel's face lit up with a cheery smile. In her fifties, she was similar in age to the postmaster.

'Everyone's pleased that the bookshop is opening again. And it's always nice to welcome a new face to our wee community. Do you knit? Do you sew? We've got a sewing bee. There are lots of women that enjoy getting together to knit, quilt and sew.'

'I enjoy knitting, and quilting is something I'd love to have a go at. It's finding time for things like that.'

'Well, you'll have plenty of time now that you're living here,' Ethel assured her. 'The sewing bee is on tonight at my cottage. You should come along. The ladies are looking forward to meeting you. They've baked a cake for your arrival. We heard it was supposed to be today, but we weren't sure if you'd be here. Coming from the city...city folk are sometimes less reliable about their schedules. Always so busy, too busy if you ask me.'

3

Bea blinked. 'Baked a cake? For me?'

Ethel smiled at her curiously. 'Yes.'

What. A. Welcome.

'Keep an eye on the post office for me, Ethel, while I show Bea the bookshop.'

Ethel shook her head at the postmaster. 'Och, I'll show her the shop. I'm more familiar with it than you.' She commented to Bea. 'I'm more of a reader than he is.' She smiled and confessed. 'I'm also the local busybody, according to folk around here, and there's very little I don't know about what's going on, including the bookshop.'

The postmaster agreed with every word.

And so Bea and Ethel headed to the bookshop, chatting as they walked along.

'I hear you're from Glasgow. Worked in accounting?'

'Yes, this is a fresh start for me.' The butterflies of excitement sounded in her voice.

'You must be so excited. Owning your own bookshop and living in the cottage.'

'It's the most adventurous thing I've ever done.' Bea felt comfortable confiding in Ethel. 'I wanted to live by the sea, away from the city, a quieter life.'

Ethel's brows raised. 'I don't know about a quieter life. We're a lively lot, as you'll find out tonight at the sewing bee. I organise it these days. Although we refer to it as the sewing bee, we do all sorts of crafts including knitting.' She turned and pointed to one of the cottages situated further along the shore. 'My cottage is the pale blue one. Pop along at seven o'clock tonight. Tea, cake, chatter and gossip galore.'

Bea laughed.

'Be prepared to be the source of the gossip tonight, Bea. We want to know all about you.'

'There's not much to tell. Nothing interesting. Ten years working in accounting. A string of broken relationships. I'm not lucky when it comes to romance.'

'Few of us are. Though Acair got his happy ending, sailing off with his new bride. I've had my share of happy endings and sorry tales. Fortunately far more of the former.'

'I've had a mixed bag.'

4

'Ah, but your story is just about to start a new chapter. With any luck, there's love, laughter and friendship in store.'

'Oh, there's a black cat staring at us.' Bea saw the cat perched on the sea wall. Its collar had a little silver thimble dangling from it, and its eyes were vivid green.

'That's Thimble, the dressmaker's cat. Quite the mystery. Something else you'll find out about.'

Bea blinked — and the cat had gone.

'Where did Thimble go?'

'He'll be off to tell the dressmaker you're here. Expect an invitation for afternoon tea at her cottage. She doesn't invite many people, but Judith, her assistant, told me the dressmaker is delighted that the bookshop is opening again and is interested in meeting you. Her cottage is up there in the forest.' Ethel indicated towards the trees high on the hills that swept up from the sea. The bay stretched along a lovely area of the coast, and far in the distance she saw the outlines of islands in the glistening blue sea.

Bea smiled. An invitation to attend the sewing bee, and now the promise of afternoon tea with the dressmaker, whoever she was. Maybe Ethel was right. The quiet life she'd anticipated here wasn't on the agenda.

Bea noticed the prettiness of the cottage bookshop as they approached. Bluebells, pansies and other spring flowers flourished in the hanging baskets, and she was eager to view the back garden that was quite substantial with an array of plants and two trees, one chestnut and the other an apple tree.

'Tavion, our local flower grower, has been tending to the flower baskets and the bookshop garden.'

'That's very kind of him. The flowers are lovely.'

'Are you green fingered?' Ethel asked.

'I don't know. I've never had to tend a garden, though the notion appeals to me.'

Ethel tilted her head and gave Bea a curious look. 'But what about the pressed flower books? How will you fulfil the orders for them if you're not familiar with flowers?'

Ethel's tone had no hint of accusation. Her concern was genuine.

'The pressed flower books?'

'Didn't the estate agent mention those to you?'

'No, not a word.'

Ethel bit her lip. 'The pressed flower books saved the bookshop from going out of business.'

'They told me the bookshop was making a profit, nothing that would make me rich, but it wasn't teetering on the brink of bankruptcy.'

'Not now it isn't, but two years ago the sales dipped and Acair thought he'd have to close the bookshop. Then most of the local businesses started to perk up, benefiting from online sales. We all started having websites and began selling our products far and wide. But the bookshop was still in jeopardy because there was nothing special about it. The books were lovely, it had a wonderful selection, but so do other bookshops. Then the dressmaker gave Acair a pile of books containing flowers she'd pressed within the pages. They were beautiful. The flowers were from her garden. Apparently she'd pressed them to preserve their beauty at the end of the summer and by the autumn they'd dried to perfection within the books. Some were well filled and others were only between each chapter.'

'What happened to the books?'

'Acair advertised them on his website and they were an overnight success. Suddenly, his bookshop was getting orders in for the books, and his other book sales flourished. Now he has so many regular customers the bookshop is doing just fine. But it was the pressed flower books that were the spark that reignited interest in his shop.'

'Am I expected to buy more of these from the dressmaker?'

Ethel shook her head. 'No, no. Acair started making them himself, using flowers from the bookshop's garden, and from other local sources. We assumed you'd continue doing this.'

'I'll definitely give it a go. I do love flowers. But I'd need to know how to press them, and what type of books to use.'

'I can help you there, and so can some of the other ladies you'll meet at the sewing bee. We all mucked in to keep the online book sales going, especially Aurora. She updated the website, and her and I dealt with the sales. Aurora was originally from here, then had a career in London working for magazines. But she's moved back and started up an online sewing, knitting and craft magazine. It's become very popular and we all contribute patterns, recipes and craft features for it.'

6

'I noticed the website was being updated but the actual shop was closed. I assumed it was Acair keeping things going until I got here.'

'No, Acair has his new wife and new life in Dundee. We offered to do this. But we all have our own businesses to attend to during the day, so night–time was when we were free. We popped along and packed the book orders. The postmaster arranged for the courier to pick them up weekly. It wasn't too much fuss between several of us. We just couldn't man the shop during the day.'

'Will the courier service still be available for me to use?'

'Yes, with many of the local businesses doing online sales now, the courier picks up our orders from the post office three or four times a week. He makes deliveries too.'

Bea smiled. 'That will be so handy. And I like the idea of the online magazine.'

'We've all benefited from the features we contribute. It's a great form of advertising to promote our products. It's a monthly magazine. I'm sure Aurora would like to do a feature on you and the bookshop. Maybe include the pressed flower books. People would enjoy reading about those, and it would help to establish you as the new owner.'

'Yes, that sounds great.'

'You'll meet Aurora at the sewing bee tonight. I'll tell her you're interested.'

They were nearly at the door of the bookshop when Bea saw a man watching them. Unlike the cat, he didn't vanish in the blink of an eye. He was quite forceful in staring over at her. He was gorgeous though, despite the intense look he was giving her. His broad shoulders were emphasised by the rugged but classy jumper he wore with the sleeves pushed up revealing his strong forearms. He had long legs and an athletic build and wore stylish cord trousers in a muted tone. A shock of golden brown hair shone in the sunlight, and even on a mild spring day, he had a look of summer about him. Behind him, a boat was anchored in the harbour, and she wondered if it belonged to him. It looked like an expensive boat, a yacht used for leisure, rather than a working boat belonging to the local fishermen.

'We're being watched again,' said Bea. Though glowered at was more apt.

7

Ethel jolted at the sight of him and linked arms with Bea, pulling her towards the bookshop. 'Don't look over at him. Smile, pretend you didn't notice him staring at you.'

Bea went to glance over her shoulder, but Ethel gripped her tight and squeezed her arm. 'Trust me. Don't look. Hurry up and open the door. I'll explain once we're inside.'

Bea fiddled with the keys, trying to find the one for the front door, and finally unlocked it.

Ethel hurried inside, taking Bea with her.

'Close the door,' Ethel whispered, feeling the urge to keep her voice down even though he was too far away to hear her.

Bea peered out the window. 'Who is he?'

Ethel tugged her back. 'He's got eyes like a hawk. Keep out of view until he gets on that boat of his.'

So it was his boat. Bea stepped back, but continued to peer out at him over the books in the window display. She too found herself inclined to whisper. 'Is he a troublemaker?' She couldn't think of what else he might be.

'Trouble for you.'

Bea frowned. 'Why?'

'That's Lewis. He's sexy, single and keeps himself to himself. Which is fine. If he doesn't want to mingle with us, that's his prerogative.'

'What's that got to do with me?'

'He wanted to buy the bookshop. But he was too late with his offer. You'd already snapped it up. It was his own fault. He didn't know the shop was for sale until he'd missed his chance. He should've been more friendly with people around here and he'd have known it was available. But oh no, he was running at the last moment, making a bid for it, saying he'd outbid everyone so he could get his hands on it.'

'So that's why he's not happy with me?'

'I've never seen him bouncing with happiness. He's a loner, a serious sort. Too intense for my liking. They say it's because of his artist nature, but no one really knows him that well. He's not from around here. He's from the Isle of Lewis.'

'Thus his name?'

Ethel nodded. 'His parents live there. He sails over from time to time to sketch and paint the scenery. He comes from money, but he's

8

also a successful artist. His paintings are exceptional. Summer is when he usually pops over, but he arrived in the winter this time to paint the seaside snowscapes.'

'Snow by the sea? That sounds wonderful.'

'It is. We get snow every winter, starting around Christmastime, right through into the New Year. The snow covers the landscape, from the forest and fields right down to the shore. It tips over on to the sand and the sea. It's quite magical. The bay helps to shelter us from the raging storms that roar along the coast, and seems to create a hub for the snow to fall and last.'

Ethel reached up and picked a book from a shelf. 'This isn't for sale. It's a photo album that shows the seasons here.' She flicked through it and stopped at a selection of pictures. 'This is the snow in winter.'

Bea studied the pictures, recognising the bookshop, other shops, and the esplanade with the harbour. 'The seashore covered with snow is beautiful.'

'You can have a look through the other pictures later.' Ethel put the book back on the shelf.

'If Lewis is wealthy and a successful artist, why did he want to buy the bookshop?'

'He rents accommodation when he's over here. Temporary leases or holiday lets. But now he's thinking of settling here on the mainland instead of going back to the isle. Cottages and farmhouses occasionally become available, but not too often. Most are inherited by family. The bookshop cottage was a rare gem. Lewis had the money to buy it, and it would've suited him being right near his boat in the harbour.'

'Would he have converted it back into a cottage and got rid of the bookshop?'

Ethel shrugged. 'We don't know for sure. He'd probably have kept it as a shop with some token books, but used it to display his artwork. Something for his own convenience and not for the community. This is the only bookshop in the area.'

Bea glanced around and felt glad that the bookshop hadn't been lost in favour of Lewis' selfish plans. She saw him climb onboard his boat and disappear below the deck.

Ethel took a clearing breath. 'Anyway, enough about Lewis. We don't want to let him spoil your first time getting acquainted with the shop.' Ethel looked around proudly. 'Well, what do you think? Is it everything you imagined it would be?'

Bea sighed and smiled.

The scent of the bookshop was as she imagined it would be. Comforting and full of promise.

The shelves were tidily stacked with an interesting range of books, from old editions and well–loved classics, to popular genres of every kind. Everything from the shelves, display units, floor and counter were made of wood and created a warm glow to the shop along with the lantern style wall lights and vintage lamps with glass shades.

Bea gasped as the realisation sank in that she owned it. 'It's the most beautiful bookshop I've ever seen. And so tidy.'

'Acair was a fusspot when it came to keeping the bookshop tidy. But there are times when being fussy pays off. The bookshelves were always kept neat. He cleaned everything down before leaving. We helped, but his bookshop was always free of stoor and sticky finger marks. All his account books are under the counter and you'll have access to the website with the data, inventory and accounts on there. I'm assuming you're au fait with things like that with you working in accounting and finance for years.'

'I am.' It was one thing she was sure about tackling. Often the paperwork side of running a bookshop could prove a challenge, but Bea had a great aptitude for balancing accounts. 'I'm fortunate to have a knack for numbers.'

'I have to do my own business accounts. I could see them far enough.' She shrugged. 'But I do them and keep things right.'

'I've always liked the assurance of numbers. They either add up right or they don't. No ambiguity. They're reliable. You know when they're correct or not.' Unlike people, she'd often thought, whose loyalty, trustworthiness and dependability fluctuated wildly.

One remnant of Christmas remained — a piece of tinsel beside the till.

Ethel picked it up. 'We helped Acair to pack the decorations away. We must've missed this piece. It belongs in the Christmas box upstairs in the nook.'

'The nook?'

'I don't think Acair filmed that when he made the video for the estate agent to advertise the premises. I think you only viewed the virtual tour of the bookshop.'

'Yes, I did. The description and the bargain price of the shop caught my interest immediately. Then when I saw the video I was so taken with it I couldn't wait to buy it.'

The virtual tour had shown the bookshop that occupied the entire front part of the cottage. Comfy chairs were tucked into two alcoves, and there was an unhurried ambiance where browsing was encouraged. Every available space was filled with books, from the latest hardbacks to second–hand paperbacks and collector editions. An enticing selection of fiction and non–fiction books were displayed in the window.

Then it showed the homely cottage comprising of a living room, two bedrooms, bathroom and kitchen. The living room and kitchen both opened out on to the garden, and she'd pictured herself standing there, breathing in the scent of the flowers mingling with the sea air. The bedroom windows were at one side of the cottage, with the frosted glass bathroom window on the other side.

'I'll give you a rundown of the bookshop. Years ago, I used to help Acair when he was busy. I've always been a bookworm. If I hadn't ventured into spinning and dyeing my own yarn for knitting, I'd have loved to have worked here.'

'You make your own yarn?'

'Yes, I run my wee business from my cottage. I'll let you have a go at the spinning tonight. If you're a knitter, you'll enjoy it.'

Bea smiled in anticipation. 'I love yarn. Even if I wasn't a knitter, I think I'd still buy new balls and skeins of it just to admire the colours and texture.'

'I know exactly what you mean. I'm the same with fabric when it comes to sewing and especially for quilts. Most of the ladies at the bees have yarn and fabric stashes. Far more than we'll ever use.'

The easy friendship that Bea felt with Ethel deepened over a chat about yarn and knitting.

'I'm not an expert knitter,' Bea confessed.

'I'm betting you made that lovely scarf you're wearing. That's snowdrop stitch if I'm not mistaken.'

'It is. I learned it online and knitted this during the winter. And I've been admiring your lavender cardigan since the moment I saw it. It's gorgeous. I love the colour.'

Ethel seemed pleased. 'Lavender, lilac and tones of sea blues are the colours I'm promoting this season. But I have to admit, I love lavender. I'll bring samples of the new yarns for you to have a go at tonight. Bring your own knitting along though.'

'I'm not really working on anything at the moment. I was bogged down in work for the finance company and spent most of my time trying to get out of the bit and catch up on my reading.'

'Oh, that's even better. You can start knitting something fresh. Just bring yourself along tonight. And pretend I never told you about the cake.'

'I promise to be surprised.'

They laughed and then Ethel pointed to the stairs that led up to the nook.

'Come on, I'll show you the nook and then give you a tour of the cottage itself.'

CHAPTER TWO

The Cosy Cottage

With Ethel leading the way, they went upstairs to a small loft conversation that housed a private area where the pressed flower books and other knick–knacks were stored.

Bea liked the feel of it instantly. 'It's so cosy and feels like a secret nook away from the world. Very tidy, just like the shop.'

'Acair worked on the pressed flowers up here. Those are a pile of romance books that were intended to be used next.'

Bea picked up one of the romances. 'Won't the flowers ruin the book?'

'No, they enhance the experience. Give something extra. The romances are popular paperbacks that can be bought easily, so they're not limited editions or anything like that. But if you pop a sheet of baking paper between the pages before adding the flowers, no mark is made. Although I have to say I quite like the effect where the flowers are pressed straight on to the book paper.'

Ethel opened one of the pressed flower books. The flowers had dried and their colours were muted, but they'd retained their floral beauty. 'See, you can still read the book. The print hasn't been affected, though some pages have a sort of vintage quality where the outline of the flowers can be seen on the lettering. I love that.'

Bea opened one book with the baking paper protecting the pages and one without. 'I like both, though there's something ethereal about the pages where the flowers have left a hint of themselves on the words.'

'That's what I love, and the scent. It reminds me of the past. A mild fragrance of flower petals or summertime by the sea.'

Bea ran her hand along the antique writing desk where the romance novels were neatly stacked. 'This is a great desk.'

'There's another small antique writing desk in the cottage living room. Acair set his laptop on it. The perfect blend of vintage and modern.'

'Was he into antique furniture?'

'The cottage originally belonged to his grandmother. He was brought up by her, the only family he had left. She decided to have the cottage converted into the bookshop. She was a bookworm and thought she could make a living from the shop. And she did. Acair worked with her, and he inherited it from her later on. The furniture in the cottage is a mix of old fashioned and modern. Acair's grandmother had a love of florals, and that's why there's a touch of flowers in the decor and styling.'

Bea admired the desk. A few marks indicated it had been a working desk throughout the years. 'It's well used but looked after.'

'So is the other desk. I prefer when there's a bit of wear on them as I don't feel so precious about using them.'

Bea picked up a roll of baking paper and noticed the scissors were ready to snip it to the right size and insert between the book pages. 'Do I have to do anything special with the flowers before I press them?'

'Pick what's pretty, nothing too big or bulky. Pansies, daisies and violets are ideal. Use fresh flowers without dew or rain on them because you want them free of moisture, nice and dry. Shake them clear of dirt and make sure there are no wee beasties hiding in them.'

Agreeing that Bea would learn to make the pressed flowers books, they went back downstairs and through to the cottage where she would live. Pressed flowers in glass frames decorated some of the walls.

'Acair must've had a hard time leaving here,' Bea said, feeling at home.

'He told me it was time to leave.'

'I suppose getting married changed everything.'

'He'd always loved her. They'd been sweethearts when they were young. She hoped he'd marry her, but being inexperienced he dragged his heels, so when her family moved away to Dundee she married someone else. The marriage didn't last, and in less than two years she'd been married and divorced. The whole bitter experience put her off marriage. She said she'd never marry again, despite her mother, sisters and aunties encouraging her to wed Acair. They loved him. He's a sweet–natured man, cheery company, and quite good looking.'

'What made her change her mind?'

14

'Time and circumstance. They kept in touch. Then one day when he asked her, she finally said yes. I remember how happy he was. He set about unravelling himself from his past, selling the bookshop, marrying the love of his life and moving to Dundee. Apart from taking a load of his favourite books with him, he the left the cottage furnished.'

Bea looked wistful, grateful that she'd been the one to buy the bookshop and that he'd left the fittings behind.

'The women in her family adore him. Acair will be spoiled rotten.'

Bea smiled and looked around the living room. It was light and airy with classic floral print comfy chairs and sofa. The original tiles around the fireplace had a bluebell print and the white walls were offset with the glow from cosy lamps and pretty curtains.

'Everything's been cleaned and the sewing bee ladies have gifted you a new quilt.'

A handmade quilt was folded neatly on one of the chairs. It was made from floral print fabric. Bea pictured snuggling under it in front of the fire.

'That was so kind of them.'

Ethel glanced around the living room. 'You'll probably want to redecorate the cottage to your own taste.'

'No, this is perfect. Far better than I could do.'

Messages started to sound from Ethel's phone. She quickly checked the messages. 'It's several of the sewing bee ladies. Word has got around that you're here. I have to call Hilda. She says it's a cake emergency.'

Bea nodded and wandered over to the writing desk bureau, picturing it would be ideal for work. She liked that it had little dookits for keeping letters, and a pull down fall to set her laptop on.

'Hilda, it's me. Yes, she's arrived. A lovely young woman. She's coming along to the sewing bee tonight. Her full name?' Ethel waved to Bea for her attention, but didn't let on to Hilda that she was there. 'I don't think she'll want her full name iced on her cake. Beatrice?'

Bea shook her head adamantly and mouthed — *just Bea.*

'No, just Bea. B...E...A. White icing is perfect. Okay, I'll let you get on before your mixture dries up. See you later.' She clicked the phone off.

Bea stood wide–eyed eager to hear what was going on.

Ethel smiled at Bea. 'Hilda is icing your name on the cake. She'd made extra icing in case you wanted the full lettering.'

'I didn't expect the ladies to go to all this trouble for me. I hope Hilda hasn't wasted her time making extra icing.'

'No, she says she'll ice her macaroons with it.'

Ethel began showing Bea around the cottage and explaining how to light the real fire with kindling when there was a thunderous knock on the front door of the bookshop.

Bea and Ethel jumped, startled by the intrusion.

'Could it be a customer thinking the bookshop's open?' Bea sounded nervous. She wasn't ready to deal with customers yet.

Ethel peered into the shop, shook her head and whispered urgently. 'No, it's Lewis. How dare he interrupt us. He knows fine you're just getting to grips with the bookshop.'

His insistent fist hammered again on the shop door.

Bea peeked out, but Ethel pulled her back. 'Don't let him see us,' she whispered.

Bea nodded. 'I saw him go below the deck of his boat, so he won't know for sure whether we're in or out. We could've left when he was scrubbing his portholes.' 'We'll pretend we're out,' Ethel whispered, taking a sneak peek through the shop to watch Lewis who was now cupping his hands on the window and staring in. 'He's got a face like thunder.'

Bea took a deep breath. She'd had to deal with awkward men at work lately, especially when she'd told her bosses that she was handing in her notice and moving to the Highlands to run a bookshop. Their sneers were forged into her mind forever. So she wasn't in the mood to hide away from Lewis.

'Let me tell him to go away. The bookshop is mine and whatever problem he has with that, he can stick it up his—'

'No, bide your time.' Ethel grabbed Bea's arm, preventing her storming through to the bookshop to give Lewis a telling off.

Lewis knew they were hiding in the bookshop, pretending they weren't in. Not one hundred percent certain, but pretty sure.

Giving a glance over his shoulder that would've wilted less sturdy flowers in the hanging baskets, he marched away and headed back to the rented cottage he was living in further up in the forest.

Two sets of eyes watched through the bookshelves as he stomped off.

'He's definitely got a burr up his bahookie,' said Ethel.

'Or needs one,' Bea added, sounding feisty.

They started to giggle and then broke into laughter.

'Wait until the ladies hear about this tonight.'

'Scandalous gossip,' Bea chimed–in.

'Oh, there's always lashings of that around here,' Ethel confirmed with joy.

And then they laughed again, filling the bookshop with their triumphant giggles.

Ethel showed Bea how to work the till, the bookshop's accounts, ordering and other aspects and then left her to familiarise herself with everything.

'I'll see you later at the sewing bee. You've got my number. Phone if you need anything,' said Ethel.

Bea waved her off. 'Thanks for all your help.'

She locked the door to prevent Lewis barging in, and gazed around the bookshop. It was hard to believe she'd done what she'd set out to do, to buy the bookshop and start afresh in the Highlands. The day wore on as she settled in.

Bea was all alone in the bookshop, but not lonely. She could never be lonely surrounded by hundreds of different worlds and thousands of characters she'd yet to read about. She never felt alone when she had a book in her hands, and lately she'd rarely been without one or two stories on the go as life trudged on around her.

Despite the work to be done and the things she had to learn, she was determined to make a great job of it. She nodded to herself. Yes, it was definitely time to make a new life for herself here, amid the shelves of books, all neatly stacked and accounted for.

The bookkeeping side of the business didn't concern her. Accounts and paperwork had been part of her job for years. Thankfully, everything seemed in order and with Acair being a fusspot, her main task was to familiarise herself with the books for sale.

If she hadn't promised Ethel she'd go to the bee, she'd have enjoyed the entire evening looking at the books. But the bee wouldn't run too late, so after meeting the ladies and getting some knitting done, she'd have time before bed to study the books.

She unloaded her car that contained everything she owned, brought her bags inside and piled them in the hallway.

She'd unpacked some of it when she realised there was no food in the kitchen, so she decided to pop to the grocery shop near the post office and pick up some shopping. She'd only had cups of tea, and the time had flown in.

Grabbing her purse, she hurried outside, locked the door and headed for the shop.

A calm twilight stretched along the shore and the colours of the sky, from pink to lilac, cast the sea in a shimmering glow. If she hadn't been in a hurry she'd have walked the length of the esplanade and soaked in the beauty of her surroundings. There would be other nights she assured herself as she disappeared into the shop.

She bought fresh milk, bread, cheese, pasta, tinned goods and a selection of vegetables including carrots, onions and potatoes with the intention of cooking a hearty dinner. She'd hadn't eaten anything all day and her stomach was rumbling. She liked to cook, and bake, and the kitchen had everything she needed from pots and pans to plates and cutlery, all cleaned and ready for use.

By the time she walked back to the bookshop, the twilight had deepened to a burnished bronze and the air had a colder bite to it. Winter had gone and spring was certainly here, but the sea air was quite brisk.

She hurried into the bookshop with the intention of lighting the fire and making herself a hot cup of tea.

With a tasty dinner cooking on the stove, she unpacked the rest of her belongings and tidied them away. She owned no furniture in her flat in Glasgow, so the move was easier than she'd anticipated, especially when she discarded what she didn't need from her past to start a new life. Clothes, her favourite books, personal possessions and her laptop were neatly added to the contents of the cottage.

While busy in the kitchen she looked out the window at the garden realising she hadn't even peeked at it. Although it was now early evening, she opened the kitchen door and lit the hanging lantern that illuminated the garden right down to the trees at the bottom of it. A lavender hedge separated her garden from the field.

A breeze blew through her hair, causing her to shiver, but she was excited at the prospect of having a garden to step out on to. What a difference it would be living here instead of residing in a city flat.

She wrapped her arms around herself for warmth and had a quick look, wandering across the lawn and imagining that the flower beds would soon be blooming with flowers. There were already daffodils, bluebells, crocus and pansies, and blossom on the apple tree.

She gazed up at the sky, so clear with a hint of stars, and felt grateful for her circumstances, even though there was a ton of work to be done to make the bookshop thrive again after being closed during the heart of the winter.

As she walked back up to the cottage to flick the lantern off, a man's voice called out to her from beyond the trees and lavender hedging.

'Bea!'

His strong tone startled her, and she glanced down towards the chestnut tree to see Lewis standing in the adjoining field, separated only by the hedge.

She blinked. Hearing him use her name jolted her senses.

'Can I talk to you?' His voice sounded clear in the night air. 'Before you fall in love.'

She frowned. 'With you?'

A smile almost broke free from those firm lips of his, but he hid his amusement and replied, 'No, with the bookshop. I've heard that bookworms, like you, have an extreme affection for bookshops. I'd like you to hear me out before you become too attached to it.'

'I won't be persuaded to sell it if that's what you're thinking.'

His reaction showed this was exactly what he was thinking. She stood firm, waiting on his response.

'I'm prepared to pay you well. You'd make a substantial profit.'

'The only profit I'm interested in is the one I intend making from running the bookshop.'

'You won't be persuaded at all?' There was a hint of arrogance in his voice.

'No, not in the slightest.'

She heard him sigh even from this distance. 'So I'm too late?' He shook his head wearily. 'That's why I wanted to speak to you earlier when you were hiding inside the shop with Ethel.'

19

She didn't address his accusation. 'You were already too late. I fell in love with the bookshop the moment I saw it advertised and decided to buy it.'

In the lantern light she saw the muscles on his handsome face tighten. 'You're very stubborn, aren't you?'

'I can be, when riled, especially by an arrogant man who assumes that he can buy what I've always dreamed of owning by dangling money at me.'

'It's not an unreasonable offer, Bea.'

She wished he wouldn't say her name. It sent tingles of excitement through her, though perhaps she was confusing the effect he had on her with rage. How dare he stand there looking so handsome and manly.

'It's highly unreasonable to be creeping about in the bushes at night and popping up to frighten me.'

He scoffed. 'You don't seem in the least bit frightened. You seem quite feisty.'

'Then perhaps you should take that as a hint to leave me alone.'

For a moment she thought he was going to step over the hedge into her garden. She glanced at the kitchen door, estimating how fast she could make a run for it, dart inside and slam it in his face. Pretty fast. Though her fluffy slippers could slow her down.

'Stay where you are. Do not come into my garden,' she told him firmly.

'I just want to explain what I'm prepared to pay for the bookshop.'

'Prowling in the shadows and shouting at me isn't the way to go about it.'

He stretched out his arms, palms up. 'I tried to knock on your front door earlier, but you preferred to hide inside, squirreled behind the bookshelves peering out at me.'

'I wanted to enjoy the experience of my first time in the bookshop. Instead it was tainted by you and your selfish arrogance.'

The snippiness in her voice rang clear in the night air.

Her words and message didn't miss him. Was that a hint of guilt when he realised he'd spoiled this for her?

'Are we having our first fight?' His tone was level.

'Our first and last.' She doubted it, but was determined not to be beaten.

The fitting jumper he wore displayed his broad shoulders and manly chest. She was trying hard not to be affected by him. But everything about Lewis affected her. He was too sexy for his own good, for her own good, and she was mentally kicking herself for the fluttering of her heart.

He ran his hands through his silky brown hair in frustration, not knowing how sexy this was.

'I just wanted to talk to you, Bea.'

'How long have you been lurking there?'

'I wouldn't call it lurking. I saw the cottage lights were on and you seemed to be busy in the kitchen. I was trying to think whether to knock on your door again, but you came out, lit the lantern and then...well, we started arguing.'

The aroma of her dinner wafted out from the kitchen. 'I'm cooking dinner, so you can leave now — and I don't want you skulking around in my bushes again.'

He took the telling off on the chin and didn't argue back.

Bea turned and marched back inside as purposefully as her fluffy slippers would allow.

She closed the kitchen door and leaned against it to steady her nerves, then saved the pot of boiled potatoes from burning on the stove and served up her dinner.

The encounter with Lewis had curbed her appetite, but she ate a fair amount of mashed potatoes before getting ready to head to the sewing bee armed with more gossip to tell Ethel and the other women.

CHAPTER THREE

Knitting and Gossip

Ethel's eyes widened. 'Lewis was lurking in the lavender?'

'He was,' Bea confirmed. She was sitting amid the other women in Ethel's cottage. The traditionally built cottage was one of the oldest in the area. Flowers grew around the front door and the garden was filled with spring blossoms.

The sewing bee was held in the living room, and the members, all women, were sitting stitching and knitting. An extension had been built from the living room into the back garden. The extension gave Ethel more room for her yarn business. Shelves were filled with a wonderful range of yarn and knitted items including shawls, cardigans and scarves.

Bea sat beside the cosy fire telling them what happened with Lewis. Introductions had been made when Bea arrived, and like her instant friendship with Ethel, she was welcomed into the hub of the sewing bee. The easy–going atmosphere was a delight and a relief, because as she'd walked to the cottage carrying her knitting bag, she was worried that she'd be viewed as an outsider. But the opposite was true. The women were so friendly and genuinely warm–hearted. She was so glad she'd joined them.

'Lewis had a nerve prowling around your cottage,' said Hilda, a quilter. She was similar in age to Ethel and they'd been friends for many years.

No mention had been made of the cake, but secret signals were flashed between the women. They were waiting for everyone to arrive before the cake was presented to Bea.

Ione, in her twenties, one of the youngest members, arrived carrying a large bag. She put it down on a table that had a white protective cloth on it already prepared for her. 'I never thought I'd be making my own wedding dress. It's so exciting.' She swept strands of her light blonde hair away from her pretty face, and her wide blue eyes were filled with glee. She unloaded the fairytale wedding dress. Two members got up and moved their chairs so they could help her stitch sparkling beads on to the bodice and hemline.

Ione noticed Bea and smiled. She took an embossed envelope from the pocket of her pale blue calico pinafore dress that she wore with a white jumper and handed it to Bea. 'You must be Bea. I'm Ione. I hope you can come to my wedding.'

Bea held the envelope in her hand and blinked at the unexpected invitation.

Ethel smiled at Bea. 'Ione is marrying Big Sam, soon. He's our local silversmith. He's very handy with his hands. Big Sam made the little silver thimble on the dressmaker's cat's collar. He's a bookbinder too. So if you ever have a special book that's battered and worn but worth keeping, he'll bind it for you. He does lovely work. Isn't that right, Ione?'

Ione gushed about Big Sam. 'He's a very talented silversmith, and bookbinding is another talent. I, of course, am biased.'

'Ione and Big Sam are a lovely couple. So that's another man unavailable,' said Ethel. 'Maybe we should encourage Lewis to stay after all?'

Bea shook her head. 'It would be better if he sailed back home.'

The women exchanged knowing glances.

'Do you fancy him?' Ione said bluntly.

'No, definitely not. No way.' Bea's insistence ignited the women's suspicions.

Several of them giggled, causing Bea to blush.

'Oh, you do fancy him, don't you?' Ethel nudged Bea, setting off the laughter again.

Bea opened the invitation hoping to avoid further scrutiny over Lewis. Ione and Big Sam's names were written in calligraphy and there were tiny fairy logos on the paper sprinkled with glitter.

Ione smiled hopefully.

'Yes, I'd love to attend your wedding. Thank you for inviting me,' said Bea.

Ione beamed. 'All the sewing bee ladies are going, so now you're one of us, you're welcome too.'

'Lewis was skulking around Bea's cottage,' Ethel told Ione. The rest of the details were explained to her.

Ione looked aghast. 'He'd no right to do that.'

The ladies nodded in agreement.

While others arrived with their sewing and knitting, Ione set her dress up along with the most dazzling array of crystal beading Bea had ever seen.

'Ione wants a fairytale wedding dress,' Ethel explained, seeing Bea blinking against the dazzle.

'You can never have too much sparkle,' Ione chirped happily.

Bea would've disagreed if it wasn't for the fact that the dress was extraordinarily beautiful. Dazzling but gorgeous.

Ione held up one of the fairy dolls she stitched and sold for a living. 'I'm aiming for this type of look, only dazzlier.'

Bea couldn't help but smile. 'I think it'll be perfect for you.' The similarity between the fairy doll and Ione was quite uncanny.

'Thank you, Bea.'

Tiree walked in carrying her sewing bag and a box of sparkling crystal beads. She handed the beads to Ione. 'The dressmaker thought you could sew these along the top edge of your bodice.'

Ione's face lit up as if she'd been given gold dust. 'Beads from the dressmaker!'

Tiree smiled and nodded.

'I know the dressmaker is said to sew magic into her dresses,' Ione began. 'But do you think there's magic in these beads?'

Tiree shrugged, but her smile encouraged this fanciful notion.

Everyone seemed happy with this.

Bea was introduced to Tiree, an attractive young woman in her thirties with long fair hair worn in a ponytail.

'Bea, this is Tiree, the dressmaker's apprentice,' said Ethel. 'Tiree moved here fairly recently from the city to work for the dressmaker, and now she's settled here permanently after falling in love with one of our local men.'

Tiree and Bea exchanged pleasantries, although no further explanation about the dressmaker's extraordinary abilities was mentioned.

Moments later, Judith hurried in. She was her late fifties with salt and pepper curls and a friendly face. 'I hope I'm not late.'

'No, we're just waiting on Aurora,' Ethel told her, and then introduced the woman to Bea.

'This is Judith, the dressmaker's assistant.'

Judith smiled brightly. 'The dressmaker has asked me to invite you to afternoon tea at her cottage. We hope you can come along soon, before you officially reopen the bookshop.'

'Yes, I'd be happy to go for afternoon tea.' Another invitation. They were piling up, but the way the ladies spoke about the dressmaker intrigued her and she was pleased to accept.

'Would the day after tomorrow suit you?' Judith asked.

'It would.'

'I'll come and pick you up around two–thirty.'

'I have a car. I could drive myself,' Bea offered.

Judith shook her head and smiled. 'The dressmaker's cottage is tricky to find. I'll pick you up.'

Bea nodded. 'Okay.'

Ethel checked her watch. 'Big Sam is due any minute. He's popping in so we can have a look to see if the pleats in his kilts for the wedding are hanging right.'

The sound of sturdy boots sounded in the hallway, followed by the strapping figure of a man, dipping his head under the doorway and standing ready for inspection.

'I brought both my kilts,' he announced. 'This one is for the wedding ceremony.' He indicated to the traditional dark tartan kilt he was wearing. He held up a bag. 'The other one is for the reception party at night.' It was a lighter version.

He twirled around, almost giving the ladies a peek below the tartan.

'It's hanging to one side,' Ione told him. 'Straighten it up.'

Big Sam gave her a sexy smile. 'Straighten what up?'

Ione gasped. 'You behave yourself.' But then she giggled. She hid the fabric of her wedding dress that she was stitching with crystals, and pointed to his sturdy torso. 'Tighten the buckles on your waist.'

He fiddled with the buckles. Without a mirror he wasn't sure if he was getting it right. 'It's a new kilt. I haven't got the feel of it yet.'

'I can't get up or I'll spill my sparkles.' Ione wanted to help him, but the white satin of her wedding dress was covered in crystals to be sewn on. And she didn't want Big Sam to see her dress before the wedding.

Ethel went over and gave him a hand. 'You need to adjust the waist.'

He put his hands out to the sides and let her sort it.

'There, that's better. Now give us a twirl.'

Bea admired the stylish kilt and Big Sam certainly suited it, but she hadn't expected he'd gone commando, and when he twirled she got a flash of his particulars.

'Oh, I think it's hanging well,' Ethel said, sniggering.

'Don't burl so hard,' Ione scolded him playfully.

He grinned and tried to twirl without revealing anything. 'Are the pleats okay?'

'Yes, very neat,' Ethel confirmed.

Tiree complimented him on his kilt. 'That's perfect for a groom to wear.'

'Yes, you suit it well,' Judith added.

Ethel introduced him to Bea. 'This is Bea. She's opening the bookshop up again. I've told her about your bookbinding.'

'Pleased to meet you,' he said.

After Ethel adjusted Sam's buckles again, he took the second kilt from the bag.

Big Sam smiled happily. 'Avert your eyes ladies and I'll put the other kilt on.'

All the women, except Bea, looked away or closed their eyes. Bea wasn't quite used to this and hesitated.

He whipped his kilt off in front of the fire, causing Bea to stare in shocked surprise at what was in full view.

'Oh, someone's seen my whistle,' Big Sam announced laughing.

Bea blushed and tried to pretend she hadn't looked. 'I didn't see anything.'

Big Sam tightened the buckles on the second kilt and then said, 'You're safe to look now.'

Amid the giggling and Bea's embarrassment, they agreed that the pleats on both his kilts were hanging nicely.

Big Sam got ready to leave. 'I'll let you get on with your sewing now.' He glanced around. 'But is there any cake going begging?' He smiled at Bea. 'Did you enjoy your cake?'

Ione and Ethel stared at him, giving him a look to keep quiet about the cake.

He got the message. 'Okay, I'll burl myself away home. Thanks for your help.'

As Big Sam left, Aurora arrived in a flurry of cheerful harassment. 'Sorry I'm late. I was updating the website for the magazine.' She was in her thirties with blue eyes and shiny chestnut hair, and although a trouble magnet, full of good intentions. She sat down and opened her craft bag. Quilting, embroidery and knitting projects were brimming from it.

Hilda crept away to the kitchen...

'Have I missed anything?' Aurora smiled at Bea. 'I'm guessing you're our new member. I'm Aurora.' She paused to catch her breath and then said, 'Why are you blushing? Are the ladies embarrassing you already with their talk of handsome men?'

'She's seen Big Sam's whistle,' Tiree revealed.

Aurora shrugged. 'Haven't we all.'

'Lewis was skulking around her cottage,' said Ethel. 'He wants to buy the bookshop.'

Aurora sounded firm. 'I hope you've no intention of selling it to him.'

'None at all,' said Bea.

Aurora pulled out her knitting. 'That's fine then. We can't let Lewis take over the bookshop and fill it with his paintings.'

'Ta–da!' Hilda announced walking through from the kitchen carrying the cake they'd made.

Bea couldn't believe the trouble they'd gone to. The cake was shaped and decorated like a book. Iced to perfection. Her name was written in white icing. She'd promised Ethel to act surprised about the cake, but there was no need to pretend.

'This is beautiful,' Bea said, smiling. 'I never expected anything special.' This was true. A vanilla sponge or chocolate cake at the most was what she'd anticipated.

'We wanted to thank you, Bea, for promising to keep the bookshop open,' said Ethel.

The other members nodded in agreement, happy that their local bookshop was part of their community again.

Hilda spoke up. 'It was very daring of you to up sticks and buy the bookshop. I admire your determination.'

Ethel poured several cups of tea and then handed the cake knife to Bea. 'Would you like to do the honours?'

Bea hesitated. 'It's too lovely to cut.'

'Come on,' Ethel urged her.

With the bee members buzzing with excitement, Bea cut it into the cake. A delicious vanilla sponge was layered with jam and cream. Bea handed pieces to the women, served up on Ethel's vintage plates.

Over tea and cake they continued to gossip about Lewis.

'That field adjoining your cottage belongs to Tavion the flower grower,' Ethel explained to Bea. 'He won't be happy that Lewis was trampling about in it.'

'A flower grower?' said Bea. 'Perhaps I can buy flowers from him for the books.'

'Yes,' Ethel confirmed. 'We've got a flower hunter too, Fintry. His cottage is nearby and his garden is amazing.' She paused. 'He's very handsome, as is Tavion, and our chocolatier, Cuan McVey. But they're all taken now.'

'So is Bredon the beemaster,' Hilda added. 'There aren't as many single men as there used to be.'

'But it's like the fields,' said Ethel. 'Different crops at different times. New men will come and stay and some of them will be single. We tend to attract slightly more mature men, in their thirties, men that are searching for happiness, even though they refuse to admit it.'

Tiree nodded. 'Teenage lads and men in their twenties tend to go away to the cities, to university, or to experience urban life.'

'Lewis is single,' Ione chimed–in as she finished her cake and began stitching the beads on again.

'But he's quite standoffish,' said Ethel. 'Very handsome though.'

Bea pretended not to be interested.

'Sexy and fit,' Aurora admitted. 'It's a shame he wants the bookshop.'

Hilda nodded. 'Lewis is a handsome one. What do you think, Bea?'

Bea sipped her tea. 'I'm not looking for romance.'

Giggles rippled through the room.

'Really,' Bea insisted.

'I'm sure you're not,' said Ethel. 'But romances blossom well in a community like this. Don't they girls?'

Everyone nodded.

As the women chatted and included Bea in all their sewing bee plans, she felt quite overwhelmed. Aurora gave her a floral embroidery kit as a welcoming gift. Hilda handed her a selection of fat quarter fabrics for quilting along with a quilt pattern because Ethel had told her that Bea was interested in learning to quilt. There were many little gifts and kindnesses given to her. Ethel filled Bea's empty knitting bag with balls of her new yarn. When they told her how happy they were that she'd joined them, she became emotional, but tried to hide it.

Hilda was hand stitching the binding on one of the quilts she was working on. She sold her quilts online as well as locally. She viewed Bea with an astute pair of eyes. 'Are you okay, Bea?'

Tears welled up in Bea's eyes. 'Yes, I'm fine. It's just that...'

'Go on,' Ethel urged her. 'What's the matter?'

'You'll think I'm silly.'

'No, we won't,' Ethel assured her.

Bea took a deep breath. 'I had failed relationships with men from the office where I worked.' She faltered.

Ethel and the others nodded encouragement.

Bea steadied herself. 'There was a ruckus with some of the women from the office. They accused me of sneckin' around with the bosses to wangle a promotion. It's not true. In the past four years I only dated two of the men. I earned my promotion through hard work.'

'I'm sure you did,' said Ethel.

'But then there was the rainy day fiasco. Was it my fault I couldn't find a parking space and had to run the length of a street in the rain when I was late for our Monday meeting?'

The ladies looked sympathetic.

Bea sniffed. 'I ran into the office, threw my wet jacket off and shook myself dry. Unfortunately, the rain had soaked through to my white chiffon blouse, giving two of the male bosses an eyeful. They said it really perked up their dreich morning.'

The ladies let her continue.

Bea looked downcast. 'This caused a rift. The women never offered me so much as a biscuit again at our tea breaks.' She looked around at them. 'And here you are, baking a cake for me and making me feel welcome.'

'Those women don't sound very nice,' Hilda commented.

'We never really shared the same interests,' Bea explained. 'They were all social butterflies. I preferred staying in after work, reading books and knitting.'

'Well, you're here with us now,' Hilda assured her.

Ethel poured Bea a glass of what looked like red wine and handed it to Bea. 'Get this down you. It'll make you feel better. It's my homemade ginger wine.'

Bea accepted the glass and drank some of it. 'Wow! What's in this? It's strong stuff.'

'Extra raspberry essence,' said Ethel.

Hilda gave Ethel a disapproving stare.

Ethel sighed. 'It is ginger wine, but I added a splash of rum to it.'

Hilda raised her eyebrows. 'More than a splash, and there's whisky in it. Your ginger wine is potent, Ethel.'

Bea drank the remainder of it and seemed to perk up.

'Feeling better?' Ethel asked.

Bea blinked. 'Yes, a lot better. Sorry if I got a bit emotional. It's been a hectic time for me recently.'

Ethel topped up Bea's empty glass.

After finishing her second glass, Bea's cheeks were flushed, but she was smiling happily.

Ethel fanned her with a knitting pattern. 'Want to have a go at spinning the yarn?'

Earlier, Bea had eyed the spinning wheel that Ethel had set up for her with yarn, wondering if she could manage to try her hand at it. Now, she felt confident to give it a real go.

'Lead the way, Ethel,' Bea announced.

Although Bea got her yarn in a fankle, the ladies were impressed that she gave the spinning a go.

'It takes practice,' Ethel told her. 'You can have a shot again another time.'

The evening was filled with cheerful chatter, Ethel's ginger wine, exchanging patterns and gossip, and then they all started to pack their sewing and knitting away.

'Thank you, Ethel, for inviting me,' said Bea.

Ethel smiled. 'You're very welcome, Bea.'

The women headed out, but when the fresh sea air hit Bea, she really felt the effects of the potent ginger wine.

'Are you sure you're feeling okay?' Ethel asked her, seeing her cheeks flush.

'Oh, yes. I'm feeling...quite perky.' Bea sounded full of vigour.

Some of the other women were feeling the same, including Ione and Aurora.

Ione glared down towards the harbour. 'The lights are on in Lewis' boat.'

'So they are,' Aurora agreed.

'I wonder if we should pop down and say night–night to Lewis?' Ione sounded mischievous.

The women giggled.

Bea nodded. 'Yes, let's go and peek into Lewis' boat and see how he likes someone prowling around his portholes.'

Aurora put her craft bag down in Ethel's hallway, and so did Bea.

'Can I leave my wedding dress here and pick it up tomorrow?' Ione asked Ethel.

'Yes,' Ethel said, encouraging others to leave their stuff safely at her cottage while they went out into the night to cause mayhem.

Giggling with their mischief making plans, Bea, Aurora, Ione, Ethel and Hilda, made a beeline for the boat.

Lewis had no idea what was heading for him.

CHAPTER FOUR

Seascapes and Snowscapes

'Shhh!' Ethel whispered as the women's giggling sounded loud in the night air.

Several sets of lips buttoned and they tried to quieten their mischievous joy.

No one was nearby to see them as the women crept up to the harbour's edge.

Lewis' boat sat in the calm water, secured to the jetty, alongside some of the working boats that were empty and in darkness for the night. The only lights glowed from inside Lewis' boat, and as the women crept closer they could see him through the cabin's windows. He was all lit up.

The moonlight shone across the sea, bouncing moonbeams into the night, and Bea thought it looked quite magical. She glanced around to see if Thimble was nearby, but there was no sign of the curious black cat.

'What's our plan?' asked Aurora, eyeing several ways to board the boat, two of them precarious and one of them very daring. The daring option appealed to her troublemaking side. She shook away the notion to swing on a rope across the gap from the harbour to the boat and land on the flat roof of the cabin. Aurora then scolded herself for that second glass of ginger wine. She knew it was a cocktail of Ethel's lavish making. She knew, and yet she drank it anyway.

'You're not thinking of doing anything daring are you, Aurora?' Ethel said, knowing her well.

'No, of course not,' Aurora lied, hoping the shadowed darkness would disguise her fibbing.

'How daring are we allowed to be?' Bea asked, sounding as if the more daring the better.

Hilda placed a calming hand on Bea's arm. 'Not daring at all.'

'No,' Ethel agreed. 'This is just a wee bit of fun.'

Bea heard what Hilda and Ethel said, and yet something in her swept their words aside. No doubt it was the three and a half glasses of ginger wine, with extra raspberry essence. It would've been four if Judith hadn't sensibly intervened and replaced the glass with a cup of tea and a digestive biscuit.

'Look! What is he up to?' Ione pointed excitedly.

They all looked, and there he was, unaware of them watching him.

Bea gasped. 'He's bare–chested. Why did he take his top off? It's not a warm night.' Though it was getting hotter by the second.

'Maybe he's getting ready to put his jim–jams on,' Hilda suggested.

The women looked at her and vetoed this suggestion.

'Okay,' Hilda revised, 'maybe he's getting dressed to go home. After all, he lives in the farmer's cottage, not on his boat.'

This idea was considered, but then Lewis took his trousers off and cast them aside.

Astonished but delighted glances were shared between the women and more giggles were stifled.

Ethel's eyes widened. 'Oh, look, he's shimmying out of his short comings.'

They watched as Lewis stepped out of his underwear.

Ione stood on her tiptoes. 'I can't see anything. The windows cut the view off at the interesting parts.'

None of them could see anything below his waist.

Hilda was going to hoist Ione up on to her sturdy shoulders, but Ethel drew the line at this. Years of doing cartwheels along the shore to challenge her sister Jessie had kept Hilda's muscles strong, and although the sisters were no longer spring chickens, they still had a lot of strength in their arms and shoulders. Jessie had won a trophy at the last summer fete, beating every man in a running contest, and winning by cartwheeling over the finishing line.

Aurora reached up and tugged the securing rope from the harbour to the boat, testing it for springiness.

Ethel pulled Aurora's hand away from the rope. 'Don't even think about it.'

Aurora sighed and wondered what else she could get up to.

Bea would've been shocked at their behaviour, but she couldn't help but smile. Last night sleeping in her Glasgow flat she pictured spending her first evening alone in the bookshop checking the inventory, not checking out Lewis' hot bod with the sewing bee ladies. Life in the city was tame compared to this fiasco. And it was a fiasco, or was going to be. Ogling Lewis could only end in trouble for all of them. She tried to care, and again blamed the effects of the drink. She wasn't a drinker. She was a tea jenny. A glass of spritzer at a special function or a dram at New Year was her limit.

Bea wondered what Lewis' reaction would be if he caught them up to no good. He'd be angry that's for sure. Then something dawned on her...

Bea grasped Ethel's arm. 'I just realised that I changed out of my top into a jumper when I was cooking dinner in the cottage kitchen.'

Ethel frowned. 'What's wrong with that?'

'I took my bra off too,' Bea added. 'I was standing there in full view of anyone lurking outside watching me.'

'Ah!' Ethel understood. 'So what's fair game for Lewis is game on for us?'

Bea nodded. 'Exactly. Unless he had the decency to avert his eyes while I put my jumper on.'

'Aye, right,' Hilda chimed–in. She pointed into the night sky. 'Is that a blue moon up there?'

'Perhaps you'd already put your jumper on by the time he was hiding in the lavender?' Aurora suggested.

Bea shook her head. 'No, he said he'd seen me busy in the kitchen. I'd changed my clothes in there because it was cosy, and I could keep an eye on my pot of potatoes so they didn't boil over.'

'Fair game then right enough,' said Aurora.

Ione climbed on to the jetty and ran alongside the boat, stopping to peer in at Lewis and then ran away again. She'd slipped her shoes off and put them in her pinafore pockets so she could run faster.

Inside the cabin, Lewis put his swimming trunks on. Thoughts of the bookshop and especially Bea kept running through his mind.

A dip in the cold sea at night would take his thoughts away from her pretty face and the way his heart felt when she stood up to him, giving him a telling off for his behaviour. She was right, of course, but few women spoke to him like that, and certainly no one had in a long time. Women generally flirted with him or flattered him. He never knew when they were genuine or just interested in his money, seeing him as a financially secure prospect.

If he seemed at times unfriendly, he figured he warranted being standoffish. Until he got to know a woman and trusted her, he preferred to keep his guard up. Though the effect Bea had on him the first time he saw her threatened to upend his plans to remain distant.

He gazed thoughtfully out the cabin windows. Maybe he should get to know her better. Perhaps he should invite her to have dinner with him. Would she accept, he wondered, or would she assume he was trying to wangle into her good books to get the bookshop off her?

For a fleeting moment he thought he saw a petite blonde, a pretty and waif–like young woman flitting past the cabin windows. He shook the notion from his mind. He was tired. It had been a long day. No fairylike figures were running amok on the quayside. He didn't believe in fairies or mermaids, or all the gossip about the dressmaker sewing magic into the dresses she made. Oh yes, he'd heard the stories about how the dressmaker had the gift, was a bit fey, and could sense things that others could not.

Last summer Judith, the dressmaker's assistant, a pleasant women, approached him and handed him a note from the dressmaker herself. He'd taken it to his boat to read in private. He still had it tucked away in his files, but he remembered the two line message:

Your paintings are beautiful, Lewis, but you should consider visiting here in the heart of winter. Your summer seascapes are wonderful, but the snowscapes are magnificent and well worth painting. It was signed by the dressmaker.

No further discussion, contact or explanation was given to him last summer. But the message lingered in his thoughts when he was back on the isle and the autumn faded to winter. One day he decided to sail back over to the mainland when he'd checked that snow had fallen. It lay thick from the forest to the fields and spilled over the coast on to the sand and the sea. It looked so beautiful and he stayed to paint the snow scenes throughout the winter, living in one of the farmer's holiday cottages.

He hadn't gone home even when the snow melted and spring arrived. He was still here now, seriously considering settling down here. If only he had a cottage of his own, like the bookshop cottage...

If he'd been more sociable he'd have heard that the bookshop was available for a quick sale. He would have bought it. But then he wouldn't have met Bea. The implications of everything he'd done played on his mind.

He sighed again. A swim in the sea was definitely what he needed.

'He's got his swimming trucks on,' Ione said breathlessly as she ran back to the women.

'Taking a night–time dip?' said Ethel.

'He does that fairly often,' Aurora reminded them. 'Not that I watch him, but so I've heard.'

Ethel nodded. 'A few of the local men like to take a daily dip in the sea. But not many swim at night. I wonder if he's feeling perturbed, thwarted at not getting the bookshop?'

While they were chatting, Bea sneaked along to peer in at Lewis. His back was towards her, a honed, lean, back with broad shoulders. She watched him run his hands through his silky hair to the nape of his neck as if he was relieving tension or trying to clear his thoughts. What was he thinking about? How to wangle the bookshop off her?

Before Bea could think anything else, Lewis suddenly turned around, as if sensing he was being watched and caught her peering in at him.

Mortified that he'd seen her, Bea ran back towards the women, hissing a warning to them. 'Lewis has seen us! Run, ladies, run!'

Taking heed of Bea's hasty warning, the women hurried away from the boat and the harbour's edge and on to the esplanade.

A quick regroup and a catch of their breath before glancing back towards the boat. Lewis was out on the deck glaring at them, and seemed to be getting ready to run after them.

'Keep going,' Bea urged them. 'Head for the bookshop!'

Without hesitation they ran like blazes, hoping to reach the safety of the bookshop before Lewis caught up with them. He wore deck shoes that enabled him to sprint up the harbour and was in hot pursuit of them across the esplanade.

Ione started to giggle, and soon the others couldn't contain their mirth.

'Don't make me laugh,' Ethel shouted. 'I'm nearly out of puff as it is.'

More giggling erupted from the women, and Bea felt her heart pounding from trying not to laugh. She glanced over her shoulder and saw the fit and determined figure of Lewis gaining on them. She fished the bookshop keys from her pocket and had them ready to unlock the door. They were nearly there, but Lewis was hot on their heels, with an emphasis on the hot. Wow! That was some physique Lewis had on him. Aside from the stern look on his face, she had no objections to being caught by a man like him.

Bea put a spurt on and reached the bookshop. 'Hurry up!' She fumbled with the keys for a moment and then clicked open the door. A rush of four other women followed her inside, and then she shut the door and locked it seconds before Lewis arrived.

The women ran through to the back of the unlit shop and peered out of the shadows at him.

'Now there's a man I wouldn't mind taking a tumble with if I was a lot younger,' Hilda remarked.

The laughter continued, and from the look on Lewis' face he could hear them.

'Oh, he looks raging,' said Ethel, giggling.

Bea caught her breath, but seeing the taut muscles and toned torso pressed against the glass door of the bookshop, her heart continued thundering, and the fluttering in her stomach wasn't just from overindulging in Ethel's ginger wine.

Aurora squinted out the window through one of the book displays. 'There's Tavion hurrying towards the shop and he's shouting at Lewis.

Ione noticed her fiancé was running along the esplanade too. 'Look, there's Big Sam!'

It appeared that Tavion and Big Sam had seen the commotion and were set to defend the ladies from being chased by a half naked Lewis.

Lewis heard them shouting at him as they hurried towards him, and he stomped away from the bookshop to address their accusations.

'What do you think you're playing at, Lewis?' Tavion's voice sounded furious.

Big Sam was still wearing his kilt and the pleats had kept their creases even after he'd galloped along the esplanade to rescue Ione.

'If you've upset my wee Ione,' Big Sam roared at Lewis, 'I'll use you as a caber and fling you in the sea.'

'Calm down!' Lewis shouted back at them, defending his actions. 'They were the ones out on the prowl tonight. I caught them peering in my boat. I was getting ready to go for a swim in the sea.'

37

'Maybe you should,' Tavion told him. 'And keep swimming all the way back to the isle where you belong.'

'I belong here,' Lewis told them.

'You've never once tried to take part in anything in this wee community,' Big Sam argued.

Tavion matched Lewis in age, height and build, but Big Sam had the edge, towering over them. Three fit men, all fired up because of the sewing bee becoming more like a girls' party night out than a hub for stitching quilts and knitting.

'I think we've caused a stooshie,' said Hilda.

'Can you hear what they're saying?' Aurora peered out at them.

'I think Big Sam mentioned something about throwing Lewis like a caber,' Ione told her.

Hilda nodded. 'Lewis didn't flinch. He seems to be meeting their objections head on.'

'Are they usually this fiery?' Bea asked.

'No, I've never seen any of them knocking heads,' said Ethel. 'The men around here are generally easy going and get along fine. We're the ones that usually cause the trouble.'

Bea looked at Ethel. 'We've certainly whipped up a storm tonight.'

'Things will calm down,' Ethel assured her. 'Tavion and Big Sam are just looking out for us. They don't know the circumstances. Once they find out we're to blame as usual, everything between the men will be fine.'

'I didn't intend to cause trouble,' said Bea.

'The sewing bee evenings are often lively,' Ethel explained. 'Tonight was just a wee bit extra exciting.'

'It keeps things lively,' said Aurora. 'I couldn't go back to a quieter life in the city.'

Happy that the women didn't blame her, Bea sighed with relief and continued to watch out the window, thinking that the men would disperse soon. But then...

Bea frowned. 'Is that the postmaster in his pyjamas and dressing gown hurrying over to them?'

'He looks like he's got a toot on,' Hilda remarked. 'He must've seen the trouble from the post office window.'

'I made that velour dressing gown for him as a Christmas present a few years ago,' Ethel remarked. 'It's nice to know he's still getting some wear out of it.'

'I hope he calms things down,' said Bea. From meeting him in the post office, he seemed to have a cheery nature, so she assumed that he'd come out to help. 'Does he live in the post office?'

Ethel shook her head. 'No, he's got a lovely house. But he'll often remember something needs done at work and pops down to the post office. It was probably to do with the courier bookings. We all rely on that service.'

Bea clicked the bookshop door open a fraction and the women gathered together, hiding out of view, while listening to what was being said.

'What's going on?' the postmaster asked, doing a speedy shuffle towards the men in his slippers.

Tavion was the first to explain. 'Lewis was chasing the ladies. They had to run to the bookshop to get away from him. I heard the ladies screaming all the way from my field.'

'They weren't screaming,' Lewis objected. 'They were roaring with laughter. Up to mischief, sneaking around my boat.'

'Is this true?' the postmaster asked Tavion. 'Did you see the ladies laughing?'

'No, I was outside my house tying up my tulips and airing my bulbs,' Tavion explained. 'But I heard them shrieking and hurried to see what was wrong. That's when I saw Lewis hot on their heels.'

The postmaster eyed Lewis. 'Where's your breeks?'

'On the boat. I was getting ready to go for a swim.'

The postmaster frowned. 'At this time of night? In this weather?'

'I had things on my mind,' said Lewis.

'It's a pity you didn't have things on to cover your particulars,' the postmaster replied. 'No wonder the women were running away screaming.'

Lewis pointed an accusing finger over towards the bookshop. 'Those women are out to cause trouble. I think they're tipsy.'

'My Ione rarely imbibes. She's happy with a coke,' said Big Sam. 'The ladies were enjoying their sewing bee night when I was there having my kilt pleats straightened. The only thing they'd been drinking was tea and ginger wine.'

'Well they seemed particularly giddy to me,' Lewis argued.

'They're a happy lot,' Tavion told him.

Lewis sneered. 'Yes, happy to run along the harbour and peer in at me in my boat.'

'They were probably enjoying the fresh sea air, unwinding after their sewing and knitting,' said the postmaster.

'Ione was stitching beads on to her wedding dress,' Big Sam added.

Tavion glared at Lewis. 'You must've done something to perturb the women.'

Lewis held his arms out. 'I didn't do anything.'

Tavion shook his head. 'No? What did you do today? Anything that they'd have reason to go prowling around your boat? If that's true.'

In his mind, Lewis rewound his encounter with Bea in her back garden.

Tavion read his expression well. 'Out with it, Lewis. What did you do?'

'I, eh...I went into your field at the back of the bookshop's garden earlier tonight,' he said. 'I wanted to talk to Bea. I saw her kitchen lights were on...'

'You were lurking in my field, in the dark, watching her?' Tavion shook his head. 'From now on, keep out of my fields, and if you want to talk to Bea, try chapping the bookshop door like a decent man.'

The ladies were listening to every word.

'The men are talking about Lewis lurking in your garden, Bea,' Ethel whispered.

The women huddled close and continued to watch what happened next...

The argument started to flare up again.

'Oh, so I'm to blame for them running amok in the harbour,' Lewis snapped at them. 'Personally, I think Ethel is to blame. The women listen to her. She probably encouraged them. They'd definitely been drinking, and we all know whose cottage they'd been in.'

Accusing Ethel was Lewis' big mistake, and even Tavion and Big Sam were taken aback when the postmaster reacted at Ethel being blamed. The postmaster had been a scrapper in his younger days and still knew how to throw a punch. Taking a swing at Lewis, he missed his opponent's chin by a whisker as Lewis avoided the blow.

Big Sam grabbed the postmaster by the cord on his dressing gown and pulled him back from following through with an upper cut. 'He's not worth punching.'

'I won't have you blaming my Ethel,' the postmaster shouted at Lewis.

Lewis held up his hands. Clearly he'd really upset the postmaster. 'Sorry, I take it back.'

Bea nudged Ethel, and the women smiled at her.

'I didn't know you belonged to the postmaster,' said Bea.

Ethel tightened her cardigan and seemed delighted. 'He's been chasing me for years.'

'Has he ever caught you?' Bea asked.

'Only a few times,' said Ethel.

'Things seem to have calmed down again,' Aurora said, watching the men go their separate ways.

Ione ran out to Big Sam. 'I'll see you tomorrow, Ethel,' she called back and waved.

Ethel, Hilda and Aurora got ready to leave the bookshop.

Aurora smiled at Bea. 'We'll chat soon about featuring you and the bookshop in the magazine.'

Bea nodded. 'Great.'

'I'll drop by in the morning with your knitting bag,' Ethel said to Bea.

'Thanks, and thank you all for the cake and the gifts,' said Bea.

'I'll bring the gifts along with me in the morning,' Ethel promised. 'Get a relaxing night's sleep, Bea.'

As they headed away, Bea waved to them and locked the bookshop door. In the distance she saw the figure of Lewis, silhouetted against the sea and sky, standing on the deck of his boat.

She stepped back as he glanced over at the bookshop before diving into the sea. She imagined the cold salt water, refreshing, yet dark and perhaps with an edge of danger and excitement. Or was she secretly picturing Lewis and how he made her feel?

CHAPTER FIVE

Bluebells and Crocus

Light from the cosy fire flickered in the hearth. Bea sat by the fireside in the living room on one of the comfy chairs sipping a cup of tea and eating hot buttered toast.

It was almost midnight. She sighed and started to unwind. What a day it had been — and what a night. An evening at the sewing bee had been an unexpected adventure.

She thought about Lewis, and her heart started to react again picturing him running in his swimwear. What a strong, lean build he had, but she couldn't dwell on thoughts of Lewis. Another broken heart was the last thing she needed, and it was obvious he was only interested in her bookshop.

She sighed again, finished her tea and toast and padded through to the bookshop in her fluffy slippers.

The lantern outside the front door gave a glow to the bookshop, and in the shadowed darkness she looked out the window at the view of the sea — and Lewis' boat. Lights shone from inside it. Was he still swimming? Was he still angry with her? She shook the questions from her mind. It was too late at night for such thoughts.

Everything was so quiet inside the shop, no sound of city traffic, noise from neighbours, and the cottage's traditional build kept the sound of the sea to a mere whisper. A soothing sound. She wouldn't miss the perpetual noise of the city.

Gazing around the bookshop she felt a sense of wonder and excitement. It was like being locked in a bookshop at night, having it all to herself, just her and all these wonderful books. But this wasn't an overnight treat, this was her future. For the first time ever she felt that her future had a glow around it. Safe from the world, surrounded by stories.

Walking around, she read the various titles, many she knew, and planned to keep the shop as neat as it was now. She preferred things tidy. Acair's range of books was an eclectic selection that matched her own taste and extended into titles that intrigued her. The less familiar titles urged her to expand her ideas. His years of honing the choice of books that customers enjoyed wasn't something she wanted to change until she'd settled into her own way of doing things.

The books in the window display were obviously suited to the wintertime market, and she'd need to create a fresh display. A springtime theme would be nice, perhaps with flowers to enhance the display and attract attention. Glancing around she started to cherry pick a few titles she thought would be ideal, and before she knew it, it was well after midnight, but the window was looking great. Another task tick boxed. In the morning she'd add fresh flowers to the display, picked from the garden.

Excitement had overridden her tiredness, but she knew she had to get some sleep.

As she went to walk through to the cottage two things happened...

One of the books toppled and fell on to the floor. It startled her, especially in the quietude when everything seemed calm. Picking it up she recognised the title, one of her favourite historical romance novels, tied with ribbon to secure the pressed flowers tucked inside the pages. The pressed flower books were stacked on a little table and she wondered why the book had suddenly tumbled. She put it back, and as she looked out the window she saw the lights go out on Lewis's boat.

Stepping back into the shadows, concerned she was lit up by the lantern, she watched Lewis, fully dressed in classy trousers and a cream cable knit sweater, jump from his boat on to the jetty and then walk up to the esplanade.

She assumed he was heading to the cottage he was staying in somewhere up in the forest. He started to walk away and then suddenly looked over, staring across at the bookshop. Had he seen her? No, she was well out of view. But maybe he sensed she was watching him. People sometimes sensed that they were being watched.

He continued on, striding away into the night and disappeared from view.

Shrugging off the feelings that confused and excited her, she went through to the living room, put the ornate guard up to keep the fire safe while it burned itself out, and climbed into bed in the larger bedroom. It had a big comfy bed topped with a duvet and patchwork quilt. Someone must have specially designed and sewn the quilt because the pattern blocks incorporated book fabric. The sewing bee ladies had probably stitched it. She wondered if she could learn to make a quilt like this.

Lying in bed, she had a view from the side of the cottage that included part of the coast, and she could see the fields and the sea. Tiny lights glittered far in the distance on the islands.

A full moon shone bright in the dark sky. Moonlight streamed through the window and cut across the bottom of her bed. She could've closed the curtains, but there was something magical about the effect it had, as if the night was sprinkling stardust into the room.

The tiredness hit her, and she fell asleep, snuggling under the covers, thinking of books and trying not to think of Lewis.

Morning dew sparkled on the crocus, bluebells and other spring flowers she'd picked in the garden before breakfast.

Up bright and early, having slept sound all night, she wanted to add the flowers to the window display. Vases were in the kitchen cabinets and she'd chosen two that had a floral print and filled them with water.

Shaking the dew from the petals, she stood for a moment in the garden and breathed in the air. If she could've bottled it as perfume the fragrance would've been amazing with top notes of the sea layered with the scent of bluebells, crocus and fresh greenery.

After putting the flowers in the window, and having cereal and fruit for breakfast, she started to deal with the online orders and was packing the books upstairs in the nook when there was a knock on the front door.

Bea hurried down and smiled when she saw it was Ethel.

'I brought your knitting bag that you left at my cottage last night.' Ethel handed her the bag along with the embroidery kit from Aurora and other little gifts the women had given Bea.

'Thank you, Ethel. Do you want to come in?'

'Just for a few minutes. I don't want to hold you up, and I've a lot of orders for my new yarn to pack for my customers.' Ethel stepped inside. 'How are you this morning?'

'Fine, I slept well. All the sea air I suppose, and the excitement.'

'I popped a jar of my homemade raspberry jam into your knitting bag.'

Bea winked. 'With extra raspberry essence?'

'No, nothing like that is added to my jam.'

They both laughed.

'I hope you don't think that last night's antics are a usual occurrence on our sewing bee nights.'

'Not at all. I'm sure other evenings will be confined to sewing and knitting.'

Ethel didn't make any promises, causing them both to laugh.

'Lewis has apologised to the postmaster, and apparently to Tavion and Big Sam.'

'Really?' said Bea.

'Yes, he was up at the crack of dawn. Tavion was working in one of his fields when Lewis apologised and wanted to buy flowers from him. Then he phoned Big Sam and smoothed things over. And he was the first one in the post office this morning. So everything's hunky–dory with them all now. Ructions don't last long around here. There's the odd stramash and then everything's fine again.'

'I'm glad. I feel responsible for what happened.'

'We all got a bit giddy, so it's not solely your fault, and it's okay now.'

'Have you seen the postmaster this morning?'

'I have. I dropped off some parcels early.' Ethel put her hand to her mouth to stifle a giggle.

'What is it?'

'Don't tell the postmaster but...I was fair thrilled that he stuck up for me last night. Taking a swing at Lewis! I knew he'd done boxing in his younger days, but I've never seen him say boo to a coo. He's a cheery sort, and it takes a lot to get his dander up.' She smiled gleefully. 'I could hardly get to sleep last night for thinking about him defending me like that. I never thought at my time of life I'd feel like a damsel in distress being protected by a man. I was all a flutter.'

Bea smiled at her. 'Maybe you'll have a happy ending like Acair and his wife?'

Ethel gasped. 'Don't even hint at that to the postmaster. He'll start chasing me again, and with my new yarn collection taking off, I don't have time to run away from him.'

'Perhaps you should let him catch you?'

'You're a bad influence, Bea.'

45

'In a good way.'

Ethel smiled. 'I'd better get going before you persuade me to do things against my better judgement.'

After Ethel left, Bea pushed on with the book packing. There was a small, folding trolley downstairs behind the counter and she put the parcels in that to save carrying them along to the post office. The hardbacks were quite heavy. These included two large cookery books filled with traditional Scottish recipes. A peek at the pudding section put her in the notion of making cranachan — delicious layers of fresh raspberries, oats, cream, honey and whisky. There was no getting away from those raspberries, she thought, and planned to buy some from the grocery shop when she was out at the post office. She also had leftover mashed potato and a mix of other vegetables including cabbage and onion, and seeing the recipe for rumbledethumps she decided she'd cook this up using Scottish cheddar and butter for her dinner later on.

The other hardback books ordered were beautiful issues of the local flower hunter's new non–fiction book about his flower hunting exploits and finds, illustrated by Mairead, a botanical artist. Mairead had moved from the city and was now engaged to Fintry the flower hunter, so another wedding was being planned.

She walked along to the post office with the trolley filled with books, and enjoyed the scent of the sea. She went inside.

'Getting the hang of things I see,' the postmaster said as Bea handed over the packages.

'Yes, I thought I'd post out some of the online orders,' said Bea.

'Any more trouble from Lewis?'

'No, and I heard he made amends for the set–to last night.'

The postmaster nodded. 'He did, so there's no bad feelings between any of us now.'

'Ethel was fair impressed by what you did,' Bea confided.

His eyebrows raised in interest. 'Was she now?'

'I didn't tell you that.'

The postmaster tapped the side of his nose. 'Thank you, Bea.'

After picking up raspberries, cream and other tasty items from the grocery shop, Bea headed back to the bookshop.

While the kettle boiled for a cup of tea, she put the shopping away. The kitchen was pretty with a mix of sky blue and cream units, an old fashioned dresser and a small table for two with chairs. The chairs had quilted cushions for soft seating.

Opening the kitchen door, she stood there, breathing in the garden air and drinking her tea. The morning sun shone in a pale blue sky and reminded her of a watercolour painting where the tones faded beautifully and merged with the garden greenery and fields beyond. Perhaps this was the type of scene that Lewis painted, though she had no idea what type of artwork he created because she'd avoided checking out his website. Heading down that rabbit hole wasn't on her busy agenda, and taking an interest in his art would surely further encourage her interest in Lewis. No, she didn't want to fan those flames. It was enough trying not to picture him in those swimming trunks, or the way he made her feel last night when he spoke to her over the lavender hedge.

Pushing images of Lewis' handsome face from her thoughts, she wondered if she should pick some flowers from the garden and try her hand at pressing them. There were plenty of spring flowers, including the pansies and bluebells that Ethel had suggested.

Finishing her tea, she lifted a flower basket from a kitchen cabinet and snipped a selection of spring flowers along with leaves and greenery. The dew had dried in the breeze and there were no beasties in any of the petals.

Satisfied she'd picked a varied selection, she carried the basket up to the nook and started to prepare the paperback books, adding sheets of baking paper between the pages where she intended pressing the flowers.

At first, the petals kept popping up and wouldn't lie flat the way she wanted them to, but with a little patience she soon found her own method of doing it. Before she knew it, she'd pressed a pretty selection of flowers into three paperback romances, tied them secure with ribbon and weighted them down with huge books.

A sense of satisfaction washed over her. A small triumph, but an achievement nonetheless. Orders for the pressed flower books were far outweighed by the standard orders for paperbacks and hardbacks, but now she had extra pressed flower books drying and ready for sale when orders for them came in.

The nook felt so cosy and secure, a hideaway from the hustle and bustle of the world, so when the knock on the door sounded from downstairs, it jarred her from her calm thoughts.

Wiping her hands from working with the flowers, she hurried down in case it was a customer. The closed sign was still on the door, but people around here seemed to have a mind of their own and no qualms about chapping on doors that were obviously closed for business. She planned to tell them politely that the bookshop wasn't open yet, but encourage them to come back when it opened in a few days time. Even thinking that this was what she intended gave her feelings of misgivings. What if she couldn't run a bookshop as well as the previous owner? Would customers compare her unfavourably? Would they give her a chance to get it up and running again?

By now there was a second knock on the door, and something in her recognised that strong, insistent tone.

Yes, she was right. Lewis was standing outside the bookshop, but he had a bunch of flowers in his hands. A peace offering, a bribe or a sneaky gift to worm his way into her good books? She didn't have time to decide before she opened the door and faced him.

Those gorgeous blue eyes of his looked at her, sending her heart rate soaring.

Calm down, she scolded herself, hoping he didn't see the effect he had on her.

'A peace offering,' he said, thrusting the flowers at her before she could refuse them.

She studied his face for any hint of a lie and found none.

'Thank you, Lewis, they're beautiful.'

'Can we draw a line in the sand and start again?' he asked tentatively. 'I think we got off to a fractious start.'

That was putting it mildly, she thought, but kept this to herself. Instead, she nodded politely and discussed the flowers. 'Are these from Tavion's field?'

'Yes, picked by him. No more trampling into his fields or encroaching on your privacy, Bea.'

The way he said her name sent tingles through her. Jeez, she needed to calm down. Unfortunately, he was one of the most handsome men she'd seen in real life. She was sure there were Hollywood movie stars that were a ten on the handsome scale, but they weren't standing facing her, smiling, asking her to be friends with him and giving her flowers.

If he sensed the turmoil of her secret thoughts, he gave no hint of it. He glanced over her shoulder into the bookshop and nodded his approval.

'The bookshop is looking great,' he said, 'and I notice you've changed the window display. It's very...*attractive.*'

Maybe she was reading things into his words that weren't there, but she felt his eyes lock on to her face as he said it.

And then she did something she had no intention of doing — she invited him in. The words were out of her mouth before she could contain them.

'Would you like to come in and have a look around?' she offered.

Lewis didn't need to be asked twice. He stepped inside and started taking a small tour of the bookshop, peering at the books on the shelves, glancing up at the stairs leading to the nook, and then he sat down on one of the comfy chairs and picked up a pressed flower book from the table.

'I've heard these are popular and helped boost the sales of the shop when it was flagging.'

'They did. The dressmaker made them using flowers from her garden, or so I'm told. She gave the books to Acair and he put them on his website. It created a spark of interest in the bookshop again and really boosted sales.'

'Will you be selling more like these?'

'I will, but they're not the main sellers now. The regular paperbacks and hardbacks are the best sellers.'

He nodded and put the book back down on the table. 'Interesting.'

He was sitting there now, quite at home, glancing around, smiling pleasantly, and she wondered what to do with him.

Another unintended offer escaped from her lips. 'Would you like a cup of tea? I was about to put the kettle on.'

'That would be great,' he replied.

She smiled tightly and hurried through to the kitchen.

As she filled the kettle she mentally scolded herself. What was she doing? First, inviting him in, and now making him a cup of tea. She supposed he'd want a biscuit with it. But that was all he was getting. Once he'd had his tea, she'd politely edge him out the door again so she could breathe without feeling she was going to blush if he stood too close to her again.

'Can I give you a hand?'

She jumped, hearing his voice behind her.

Wide green eyes stared round at him.

'I'm sure you're busy and I don't want to hold you up. Let me make the tea,' he offered.

It must've been the hesitation in her that made him think that she'd agreed to him taking over the tea making in her own kitchen, because he was now popping the kettle on to boil and setting up the cups.

She was living in an alternative universe she thought, panicking for a moment. But with a man as handsome and willing to lend a hand as Lewis, there were worse places to reside.

'Great, I'll put these flowers in water.' Even she was surprised how calm she sounded. Keep it up, Bea, she scolded herself. He'll be moving into the spare bedroom next.

She lifted a vase from one of the cupboards.

He peered out the kitchen window. 'Do you have enough flowers in your garden for the books, the right selection?'

She had to stand close to him to fill the vase with water. He was so tall, and she barely reached his shoulders. Trying to sound unperturbed, but feeling the complete opposite, was difficult, especially as he smelled so nice, freshly showered, and so well dressed in expensive casuals. She loved men in classic knit jumpers and cords. Lewis worn them well. He looked like he belonged on the front of a men's knitting pattern, or in a magazine, advertising rustic designer wear.

'I picked some flowers this morning — bluebells, crocus, small flowers. They're easier for pressing, according to Ethel and the ladies. I've never pressed flowers before. I'll snip some of these flowers you've brought, the smaller ones, and put the others in the window display. These pink tulips are gorgeous.'

'I'll keep that in mind for the next time,' he said.

'The next time?' Her high–pitched tone startled even her.

'I don't mean to be presumptuous.'

'No, I...' What? Didn't expect to be plied with florals? 'I'm sure you're busy with your paintings. These flowers are plenty,' she assured him, smiling, hoping she'd hit the right note between thanking him and keeping him at arm's length.

'I saw smaller flowers in Tavion's field. I'll ask for those next time.'

The kettle boiled and he began making the tea while Bea sorted the flowers in the vase and snipped a few. She put them on a paper towel on the kitchen windowsill to dry.

'How do you like your tea?' He called through to her as she put the tulips in the shop window.

'Strong, splash of milk, no sugar.'

'Same as me.' He sounded happy that they had similar tastes.

Bea peered out the bookshop window, hoping that Ethel, Aurora or anybody would arrive to help her, but there was no one. The local cavalry wasn't on their way.

'Do you want me to give it to you through here in the kitchen?'

She firmly buttoned her lips for fear of what she'd quip in reply to that offer.

Bea hurried through to the kitchen, smiling, trying to appear calm.

He handed her a cup of tea, and tipped his cup against hers. 'Cheers. Here's to fresh starts.'

'Cheers.' She took a sip and tried not to think how tall he looked standing there in her kitchen. She had to stand on tiptoe to reach the top shelf of the dresser, but Lewis made it look dinky. In fact, the whole kitchen had diminished in scale and was now filled by the width of his broad shoulders and manly presence.

'It's nice and cosy in here,' he said, drinking his tea and looking around.

Oh, yes. And it wasn't from the heating.

CHAPTER SIX

Florals and Shenanigans

That alternative universe kicked in again. Bea's world was now occupied by Lewis being very helpful, ensconced upstairs in the nook pressing flowers into the romance books. He was quite adept at it and making more progress than her.

On one hand, she wasn't complaining because he was a genuine help with the work. On the other hand, being tucked away with him in the cosy nook felt quite intimate — in a nice way, but also in a sense of *what are you doing?*

The loft conversion wasn't built for a man of his tall stature. Although he could sit comfortably, he had to bend his head slightly when standing up, especially in the corners of the nook where the cottage roof sloped at an angle.

There were no windows to peer out of, or for people to peer in, and this created a little hideaway safe from prying eyes.

'Your artistic streak is showing,' Bea said, admiring the way he'd added a bit of greenery to curve around a bluebell.

He smiled at her and leaned close to compliment the page of pressed pansies she was working on. 'Those look very pretty.'

Again, certain words jumped out at her, like *very pretty*, especially when he smiled at her as he said it.

Remembering Ethel had commented that she'd hardly ever seen Lewis crack a smile, she was suspicious of his ulterior motives. He'd smiled repeatedly, as if he was having a great time with her. Really? A man like him was enjoying pressing flowers?

He added a primula to a page. 'This is quite relaxing, and it's given me ideas for my paintings. I rarely paint florals, but these pressed flowers make me want to paint them in watercolours — and I mainly paint in oils and acrylics.'

Okay, so maybe he was enjoying himself, but she wondered how much tension she could take. He was relaxed while she was a contained jackrabbit. The main problem was that she was unsettled and clearly had opened her mouth and said things she'd preferred to have kept to herself — like inviting him into the bookshop, offering tea, chatting about the flowers while he made their tea. She was in jeopardy of saying something really embarrassing. The less she said the better, until he'd gone, whenever that was going to be. A peek at the time showed it was approaching lunch. If her mouth opened and invited him to stay for lunch she'd be fried by the afternoon. The stress of trying to deal with everything — the orders, the running of the bookshop, the thought of opening it up to customers and a hundred other things weighed a ton. Adding an attraction to Lewis tipped the balance into the danger zone.

'Penny for them,' he said, smiling at her while continuing to outdo her best pressed flower efforts.

Bea blinked.

'For your thoughts. You looked so intense as if you were miles away.'

Miles away would've solved everything. It was being within knee touching distance to him that was the problem. They shared the desk in the nook and his thigh had accidentally brushed against hers a few times. If she'd been wearing nylon instead of grey jeans she imagined the sparks between them would've required a call out from the fire brigade.

'I was just thinking about when I'll open the bookshop to customers,' she lied calmly.

'When do you think that will be?'

She shrugged. 'Soon. I'll probably dive off into the deep end and open in a couple of days. I'm having afternoon tea with the dressmaker tomorrow, so I'll open the day after that.'

'I admire your gumption.'

Did he mean she was reckless opening so soon?

'When would you have opened up, if the shop belonged to you?'

His firm lips pressed together thoughtfully, then he replied, 'A week to ten days, to make sure I was ready to take on such a challenge.'

'Ten days?' No wonder she pipped him to the post when buying the bookshop.

'I like to ponder things, consider my options, take things slowly.'

Hopefully that included coming back here. She needed him to saunter off and ponder his options on his boat, or in his cottage.

'I'm usually quite the sensible type, but the bookshop seems well organised and the accounts and finance side of it doesn't bother me.'

'No, of course, you having worked for years in accounting. That will come in very handy for a young businesswoman like you.'

His comment puffed her confidence and strangely calmed her down. He seemed to really mean what he said.

'Thank you, Lewis.'

He smiled at her, then held up the book he'd finished adding flowers to. 'How many of these do you need?'

'I think you've fulfilled a month's worth of orders in one morning. That's plenty. Thanks again.'

He stood up and had to slightly bend his head under one of the lower rafters as he stacked the books on a dresser in the corner.

'You're welcome, Bea.' His tone deepened and his smile faded. 'But thank you for making me feel welcome. After my behaviour yesterday, twice, I didn't deserve it.'

Her heart squeezed for a moment, realising he really meant what he said.

'I can be a little unsociable at times,' he said. 'I know that. It's something I plan on rectifying when I settle down here.'

'Why do you want to move here? I thought the isle would be an ideal place to live.'

'It used to be, for me anyway, but circumstances changed. Now, I want my own life, away from the isle and from my past.'

She waited, hoping he'd explain further, but he didn't.

He checked the time. 'I'd better get going and let you get on with your work. I hope I wasn't too much of an intrusion.'

'No intrusion at all,' she lied.

He headed downstairs and she saw him out.

'Good luck with the bookshop, Bea. You deserve to do well with it.'

He smiled and then walked away.

Was that a goodbye? She had the strangest feeling it was, of sorts. A sadness washed over her watching him walk away, not to his boat, but along the esplanade to the cottage.

A message popped up on her phone from Ethel. She read it. *Has Lewis gone yet?*

Yes, I was hoping you'd come and save me from him.

Ethel replied. *Sorry, I didn't know if you were canoodling or not.*

Definitely not!

Pop the kettle on. I want to hear all about it.

Over tea and the fresh baked scones Ethel came armed with, Bea told Ethel what had happened.

Ethel frowned. 'What's he playing at? Making the tea, bringing flowers and then cosying up with you in the nook? That man is up to mischief.'

Bea nodded thoughtfully.

Ethel spread cream and jam on her scone. 'So, did he kiss you?'

'No!'

'He made no romantic overtures at all? Not even a bum note?'

'No, Ethel, he didn't, but my goodness, he makes me feel...' Bea sighed.

Ethel nodded. 'I'm like that with the postmaster, sometimes.'

Bea sipped her tea. 'How did you know Lewis was here?'

Ethel guffawed. 'Everybody knew. The gossip went along the esplanade quicker than a wave and then Aurora told Tavion and he told the farmers, and they told—'

'Okay, so Lewis being with me in the nook is hot gossip.'

'It is. But it's great advertising for the bookshop. Everyone's happy that you're opening up. Some weren't sure if you'd sprout chicken feathers once the realisation sank in — the work needed to run a bookshop.'

'Hard work doesn't bother me. I'm used to it. The gossip and shenanigans with Lewis are what's draining the strength from me.'

'You're looking a wee bit flushed and yet pale. You must've been stressed being so cosy up in the nook while trying to hide that you fancy the pants off Lewis.'

'Ethel!'

'Well, tell me he's not gorgeous. Half the women around here went loopy when he first arrived one summer. He'd sit on the harbour wall or on the shore and paint in the sunshine. When it was extra hot midsummer, he'd sit there with his shirt off. He's so good looking, almost too good to be true. But maybe that's the issue.' She began to confide the gossip. 'I've heard that he doesn't trust women very easily. Apparently, a few of his ex–girlfriends were only after his money and the prestige of dating a successful artist who owned a fancy boat.'

'Surely not. I mean, as you say, he's handsome.'

'Hilda's sister Jessie lives on the islands, not the isle where Lewis is from, but the gossip spreads through the islands, and that's what Jessie has heard.'

'I asked him why he wanted to move here.'

'What did he say?'

'He said his circumstances had changed, and now he wanted his own life here, away from his past.'

Ethel cupped her tea and looked thoughtful. 'Perhaps he had his heart broken, or his trust broken.'

'By women that were really after his money and lifestyle rather than being in love with him?'

Ethel shrugged. 'They may have been in lust with him. But that's not the same as loving.'

Bea nodded. 'And there could be other circumstances from his past.'

'Yes, so tread carefully. But he's a wonderful artist. His paintings are lovely.'

'I've resisted checking out his website.'

'I had a nosey at it. His seascapes are my favourites. I love the colours. Turquoise, aquamarine, sea blues. I'd have one hanging in my cottage if I could afford it, but his paintings are well out of my price range.'

'I may be tempted to take a peek at his website later.'

'But don't be tempted by Lewis until you know more about his past.'

After Ethel left, Bea continued organising the bookshop. Often, a book would catch her attention and she'd pause to flick through it, mentally listing titles she intended reading when she had time.

Bea was engrossed in one book when Aurora waved in the window. Bea opened the door and invited her in.

Aurora had her laptop with her, and a camera slung over her shoulder along with a large but stylish bag filled with all sorts of items.

'Are you still interested in the feature for the magazine?' Aurora asked.

'Definitely.'

'I'm nearing the deadline for this month's issue and it would be great if your feature was included, especially as you'll be reopening the bookshop. But if you're busy I can come back another time.'

'No, I'd love to be included in the latest issue of the magazine.'

'Great. This won't take up a lot of your time.' Aurora plopped her bag down on one of the chairs and set her laptop on the counter. 'I was thinking we could do a double page spread featuring the bookshop and highlighting the pressed flower books to include the craft element. All the features are craft based.'

Aurora sounded as if the deadline was looming fast and needed to pull the features together quickly. This suited Bea. She was well up for being caught up in Aurora's whirlwind.

Sunlight was shining in the window, creating a glow to the bookshop.

'The light's good,' said Aurora, checking her camera. 'I'll need pics of the shop, you, and the pressed flower books.'

Bea had showered and washed her hair that morning and it was one of those days, despite everything, that it fell in silky waves to her shoulders. Her makeup was minimal and she wasn't sure that her jeans and jumper were a suitable look.

'If you want to change into something else and touch up your makeup, I'll take photos of the bookshop,' said Aurora.

Bea nodded. 'I won't be long.' She hurried through to the bedroom and picked a favourite blue blouse and black trousers to wear. Mascara and lipstick and a brush of her hair and she hurried back through.

'Great look, Bea. Love the blouse.'

'Where do you want me to stand?' Bea felt slightly nervous. She'd never been keen to have her photograph taken, but this would help promote her business, so she sucked up her reticence and got on with it.

'Stand right there in the middle of the shop. The light's streaming in nicely and makes the atmosphere look welcoming.' Aurora handed her a couple of books, chosen at random from one of the shelves. 'Hold these and smile.'

Bea went along with Aurora's instructions. With her background in magazines for years she trusted she'd do a fine job of the feature.

Aurora clicked off several shots and showed the small previews on the camera to Bea. 'What do you think? I think you look amazing.'

Bea was pleasantly surprised. 'You're really good at taking photos.'

'I've had plenty of practice, and you're a great subject, and the shop looks amazing.'

Aurora asked Bea to sit on one of the comfy chairs, again holding a couple of books, and snapped more pics. Then she transferred them to her laptop.

Aurora and Bea poured over the photos on the laptop screen. 'This is basically how they'll look in the online issue, only I'll crop and edit them so they'll be even more attractive.'

Bea felt so excited. 'I've never been featured in anything like this before.'

'You look relaxed and happy, and that's perfect for this type of feature.'

'Inside I'm feeling nervous,' Bea confessed.

'It doesn't show,' Aurora assured her. 'Come on, let's get some shots of you outside the bookshop. The window display looks wonderful with those flowers. Again, that'll tie in with the theme of the feature.'

Bea stood outside in the sunlight, and allowed Aurora to adjust her pose so that the books and flowers were shown to full effect.

'You're hair is shining beautifully,' Aurora complimented her. 'And I'll take a few pics of the entire front that show the hanging baskets. I'll include a varied selection in the feature, and I'll email you a copy of all the pics that you can have for your own use.'

'Really? That's so kind.'

'We all try to help each other around here. This feature will give readers something entertaining to read, create interest in the magazine and in your bookshop. Win, win.'

'Ethel said you're doing a feature on her new yarns.'

'Yes, the colours this season are sensational. I'm tempted to buy a skein in every colour. I don't know what I'll knit with them, but I just want the yarn. The textures are fantastic. Ethel's really outdone herself with this new collection.'

'She's filled my knitting bag with samples and I can't wait to have a look at them — and the embroidery kit you gave me. It's a floral embroidery kit, isn't it? Again, Ethel only dropped my bag off earlier and I haven't had a chance to see it.'

'It's a new range of embroidery patterns designed locally by one of the sewing bee ladies. It includes floral designs — bluebells, roses and pansies, a little bird that's so pretty and two lovely garland designs. The patterns are easily traced on to the fabric. Three pieces of white cotton fabric and an embroidery hoop are included along with all the thread and instructions. The kit is another feature this month, and I thought you'd like to try it. Do you like embroidery?'

'I do, though I'm a beginner level.'

'No problem. The stitches are explained and there's a link to an instruction video.'

Bea was really interested. 'Sounds great.'

'Okay, let's go back inside and take pics of the pressed flower books — with you showing readers how you press them in the books.'

Bea led Aurora up to the nook. 'I'm no expert at this.'

'No worries. I'll photograph the process, and explain everything in the editorial.'

Aurora set Bea where she needed her, holding cut flowers, close–ups of the flowers being put on the pages, some with white paper between the pages and others without.

Bea explained the details and Aurora kept nodding, asking questions about the types of flowers used, and seemed satisfied that she could write an interesting feature about it.

'I'll take a few more pics of the flowers in the books, close–ups of the ones that have already dried. They look so ethereal and wispy. And these fresh ones that you made this morning. I love the way you've trailed leaves around the bluebells. So artistic.'

'I didn't actually do that one,' Bea confessed.

Aurora frowned. 'I thought you made these.' There was no underlying accusation or disappointment in her tone. She was genuinely surprised.

Bea took a deep breath. 'I was working on them when someone offered to give me a hand with them.'

Aurora tilted her head. 'Was it Ethel?'

'No, it was...Lewis.'

There was a slight pause and then Aurora said, 'Lewis?'

'Eh, yes, he wanted to make amends for what he did last night.'

Aurora smiled and gave Bea a knowing look. 'So you and Lewis are getting along now?'

'We are. He wants to be friends.' Bea tried to sound casual.

Aurora smiled, not easily fooled.

'What?'

'Nothing.' Aurora was still smiling.

Bea started to smile too. 'I'm not getting involved with him.'

'But you like him?'

Bea blushed and didn't say anything.

'Yes, I thought so.'

And then they both laughed.

'But I've no plans to get involved with him. I'm concentrating on the bookshop.'

'If you say so.'

Aurora picked up another book. 'Did you press these flowers? I love the choice of colours.'

'No that was Lewis. And so were those.' Bea sighed. 'I made three and I've no intention of selling them as I don't think they're quite good enough. They were my first attempt and I'm sure, seeing what Lewis did, that with a bit more practice I'll learn to make them better.'

Aurora nodded and sighed. 'The thing is, I'd like to include the ones that Lewis made. No offence, Bea, but they've got a slight edge and artistry that readers will enjoy. So, I'll include some of yours, and some made by Lewis. I'll credit him. Add his name to the feature. Keep things right.'

Bea seemed happy with this idea. 'Yes, that's fair.'

'I'll even give a link to Lewis' website so people can see his paintings. Free promotion for him. And again, something craft based.'

They headed back downstairs.

'Do you want a cup of tea before you go?' Bea offered.

'Another time. I've got to get this written up. I'll email it to you so you can check the details are correct, and once approved by you, the feature will go in the magazine.'

Bea was so excited. 'I appreciate this.'

'Okay, I'm going to run. I'll email you soon.'

Bea waved Aurora off, put the kettle on for tea and heated up some hearty vegetable broth for her lunch. She'd bought it at the grocery shop. It was locally made and thick with pearl barley, split peas, red lentils, carrots, onion, turnip, leek and other vegetables and seasoning. She served it up with a sprinkling of fresh parsley and thick slices of crusty bread.

CHAPTER SEVEN

Rumbledethumps

Fuelled up on tea and broth, Bea worked in the bookshop throughout the afternoon, until the twilight descended, casting an amber shimmer across the sea.

The lamps in the bookshop provided a comforting warmth, and Bea would've happily settled down for the evening reading, admiring the new yarn and having a look at the embroidery kit.

The rumbledethumps was baking in the oven for dinner. The aroma of the mashed vegetable mix topped with grated cheese wafted through to her, urging her to close the book she'd become engrossed in, put it back on the shelf, and flick the shop lights off.

She left one lamp on and went through to the kitchen. The fire was burning in the living room and she intended having dinner by the fireside.

The wind was whipping up a storm outside, so she went through to check that the bookshop door was secure, and that's when she saw Lewis striding towards her. His hair was being buffeted by the wind sweeping in from the sea, and he was trying to shield the small bunch of flowers he was carrying.

More flowers?

He saw her and put on a spurt, running to the bookshop.

She opened the door and let him in. He brought a gust of fresh sea air in with him.

'It's going to be a wild night.' He swept wayward strands of hair away from his face. He gave her the bunch of flowers. 'Tavion was kind enough to drop these off to me. He'd heard that I wanted smaller flowers. I didn't know what to do with them. I wasn't sure if I put them in water they'd last until the morning, or whether any hint of wilting would prevent them from being suitable for pressing.'

The only thing in jeopardy of wilting was her. From the unconsciously sexy gesture of sweeping his hair back, to bringing her flowers when a storm was brewing, to simply seeing him standing there again in the shop — her heart was doing that fluttering thing.

He was looking at her, waiting on her response.

'I'll put them in water and press them later tonight,' she said.

He seemed pleased that she was happy with the flowers.

'Well, I'd better get going.' Then he added, 'Something smells tasty.'

'I'm cooking rumbledethumps for dinner.'

'Rumbledethumps! I haven't had that in ages.'

Don't do it, she warned herself, but it was to no avail because she heard the words escape from her lips. 'You're welcome to join me. There's enough for two.'

'I don't want to impose on you.'

'If you'd rather go—'

'No, I'd love to have dinner with you.'

She smiled and popped the flowers in beside the others in the window display temporarily, then hurried through to the kitchen.

Lewis followed her.

'I was about to add more logs to the fire,' she said, thinking he'd offer to do this while she attended to the dinner.

'Great.' He headed over to the sink, pushed his sleeves up and quickly washed his hands. 'You sort the fire and I'll check on the rumbledethumps.'

Bea blinked. That didn't go according to plan, she thought, watching him grab a kitchen mitt, open the oven door, lean down and check on the dinner.

He pulled the baking dish out and nodded. 'The cheese is melting nicely.' He glanced round at her. 'Do you like it golden or lightly toasted?'

'Either way,' she heard herself reply while her mind was doing somersaults.

'I'll pop it under the grill to brown it slightly,' he said.

She hesitated for a moment, and then went through to the living room and put extra logs on the fire.

'Are we eating in the living room?' he called through to her.

'I'd planned to eat dinner by the fire.'

'Sounds cosy. Ideal for a stormy night.'

This was true. But it was also disconcerting. Somehow, she'd managed to back herself into a corner again with Lewis.

She heard him bustling about in the kitchen and left him to it.

62

By the time she'd coaxed the fire to perk up, he'd browned the cheese topping, set their plates up, sliced the bread and put the kettle on to boil. If he offered to wash up the dishes, she was keeping him.

She stood in the living room doorway watching him.

He was milling black pepper on to the portions he'd dished up on their plates.

'Would you like me to help you?' she offered.

He leaned round and glanced into the living room. 'You could set the coffee table up in front of the fire. If it's too heavy I'll sort it.'

'No, I can do that.' Bea moved the table closer to the fire. There was a comfy chair on each side.

What are you doing? She chided herself. You can't let Lewis wangle his way into your life! Though, to be fair, she was the one repeatedly inviting him to stay, so she couldn't entirely blame him.

Lewis carried their food through and set it down, then brought the tea through as well. He sat in one of the chairs and seemed utterly delighted to be dining on rumbledethumps. Somehow she hadn't pictured him opting for hearty, home cooked dishes.

'This is delicious, Bea,' he said, tucking in. 'I've barely had time to eat anything all day.' He pointed his cutlery at his plate. 'This is perfect.'

Bea joined him. It did taste good. A pang of guilt hit her as she realised she hadn't fed him anything other than a cuppa and a biscuit this morning in the nook. Perhaps he'd skipped breakfast to bring her the flowers. She hadn't even asked.

He smiled at her, and she felt her heart squeeze just looking at him. The firelight highlighted his sculptured features, and he had a great smile. Again, those broad shoulders of his caught her attention as he sat there opposite her. His sleeves were still rolled up and she noticed the corded muscles on his forearms. Lean and strong.

'Aurora phoned me,' he said.

Bea looked surprised.

'She wanted to check that I was okay with her adding my name to the magazine feature. I told her I was happy to let you take the credit for the pressed flowers in the books, but she insisted to credit me anyway.'

Bea didn't know that Aurora would contact Lewis, but she was pleased that she'd asked for permission.

'You deserve the credit. Your artistic ability outshines mine.'

'You did a great job, especially as you'd never done it before. You seemed like a fast learner to me.'

'I plan to practice so I can make them suitable for selling.'

Lewis nodded firmly, as if he expected no less from her.

'Were you doing any paintings today?' she asked.

'I started a couple of new works. One on canvas and one watercolour. Those flowers put me in the notion of the latter.'

'I'll have to check out your website. Ethel is full of praise for your artwork.'

This took him aback. 'Is she?'

'She says you're very talented, a wonderful painter.'

He raised his eyebrows in genuine surprise.

'She loves your seascapes, the beautiful colours, and she'd buy one if they weren't so expensive.' Bea smiled.

He paused from eating his dinner. 'She said that, even after I'd accused her of causing all the trouble last night?'

'She did.'

He looked thoughtful, and then continued eating his dinner.

'This is tasty. Do you like to cook?' he asked her.

'I enjoy cooking. How about you?'

'I prefer painting. I always wanted to be an artist.'

'I used to dream of owning a bookshop.'

'We're both fortunate.' He smiled over at her and her heart melted a little.

He seemed calmer now, sitting with her in front of the fire.

'You suit being the owner of the bookshop. It's very you.'

'A bookworm in a bookshop.'

The storm roared outside, gathering pace.

'No swimming in the sea this evening,' she teased him.

'Nooo, though I've been caught off guard a few times when the weather changed from calm waters to a sea storm. I'd gone for a swim along the coast. I'm quite a strong swimmer. I practically lived in the sea off the isle when I was a boy. There's a terrific energy during a storm. It's invigorating. I love the atmosphere. I've sometimes tried to capture that feeling in my paintings. Never quite nailed it.'

'I love the rain. It makes everything feel cosy. I don't think I'd like to live in perpetual sunshine.'

He nodded, and put his plate aside as he finished his meal. 'We're both living in the right place then, aren't we?'

'We are.'

He looked at her thoughtfully. 'Do you suppose you'll miss living in the city?'

'No, especially as it's so beautiful here. The sea and the countryside. The best of both worlds.'

He cupped his tea and stretched out his long legs in front of the fire. His snug cords emphasised the lean muscles of his thighs. 'Aurora was telling me that she was raised here, but moved away to London and made a successful career for herself in magazine work. Then she moved back last year, and fell for one of the local men. Now she's married, settled and doesn't miss the city.'

'Aurora has been chatty.' Bea smiled to herself, picturing the quick call about his name credit becoming a lengthy conversation as Aurora told him the local news and gossip.

'It's the first time I've spoken to her, even though I was aware of her and the magazine. I suppose Ethel and Big Sam are right — I should try to be more sociable.'

'They're a very welcoming community.'

'Indeed they are.'

'I've been invited to afternoon tea tomorrow afternoon at the dressmaker's cottage. I don't even know who she is.'

'Apparently she's a bit fey, knows things, sews magic into the dresses she makes, and has a cat named Thimble. Thimble the fifth to be precise, according to Aurora.'

'I've heard the stories, but I've no idea why she's invited me.'

'Maybe it's a sort of local custom.'

Bea shook her head. 'No, she doesn't invite many people.'

'Then there must be something special about you.'

Bea brushed this notion aside. 'There's nothing special about me.'

'I beg to differ.' The look he gave her scorched her to the core.

He saw her embarrassment and quipped casually. 'Are you going to have tea with the dressmaker?'

'I am, out of politeness and curiosity. Judith is picking me up.'

'Isn't that your car parked nearby?'

'It is, but Judith insists on driving me there because she doesn't want me to become lost in the forest.'

Lewis picked up their plates to carry them through to the kitchen. 'I'll pop these breadcrumbs in a paper bag. Take it with you in case you need to leave a trail to find your way home.'

Bea laughed and relaxed by the fire while Lewis cleared away the dishes. She heard the water in the sink and efficient rumbling in the kitchen as he washed the dishes. Oh, dear, she thought. Now she'd definitely have to keep him.

He came back through and sat down to finish his tea. 'The dressmaker wrote me a letter.'

Bea was surprised. 'So you know her?'

'Never met her, but Judith gave me a letter from the dressmaker last summer.'

'Is it private or can you tell?'

'She complimented my paintings, and then suggested I should come back in the winter and paint the snowscapes.'

'And you did?'

'Yes, and I'm glad. I loved the winter scenery and the snow by the sea was wonderful to paint. It's spring now and I still haven't gone back to the isle.'

She noticed he never called the isle his home. Had something happened in his past, the change in circumstances he'd mentioned? She sensed it had and he didn't want to talk about it.

His voice interrupted her thoughts. 'Tell the dressmaker I'm grateful for her suggestion.'

'I will,' Bea promised.

He eyed the knitting bag brimming with yarn. 'Were you planning a night in knitting?'

'Ethel gave me skeins of her new yarns and I haven't had a chance to admire them yet. The women at the sewing bee gave me welcoming gifts, including an embroidery kit from Aurora.'

'If you're itching to have a look at these, I'd be happy to pop up to the nook and put the flowers into the book for drying,' he offered.

'Oh, I don't want to put you to work,' she said.

'Fair exchange for the tasty dinner you cooked.'

He stood up and seemed intent on doing this.

Bea hesitated, almost disappointed that their dinner was now over.

'Or you could bring your knitting bag upstairs and keep me company in the nook,' he suggested.

She found herself nodding and picked up the bag.

Lewis went over to the fire and lifted some kindling. 'I'll throw more logs on the fire to keep the living room toasty for later.'

The look she gave him.

'For you, not me. I'll be heading home soon. I wasn't suggesting what you thought.'

'I didn't say anything.'

'Those expressive eyes of yours enable me to read you like a book. Appropriate for a bookworm I suppose.'

Her heart thundered in her chest as she followed him up to the nook. He brought the fresh flowers and carefully dried the water from the stems and cut the heads to press into the books.

Bea sat with the knitting bag, clutching it, hoping she hadn't given him the wrong impression. But if he really could read her like a book, he'd know she'd got herself into a pickle of a situation.

'I won't be making a habit of this, Bea,' his deep voice assured her. The richness of his tone resonated in the confines of the nook.

'I wasn't...' she went to object, but then she saw the knowing look he was giving her and didn't even try to lie.

He pressed the flowers efficiently, as if he'd been doing it for years. A fast learner, or again just that artistic flair in him.

'I don't know anything about knitting,' he said, glancing at the yarn spilling from the bag. 'But those colours look intense and blend well together.'

Did she blend well with Lewis? Anyone would've taken them for a couple as they appeared to be comfortable in each other's company, even though her heart still wouldn't calm down when she was near him.

'Ethel dyes her own yarn,' Bea told him, taking the samples from the bag and letting him view the colours and textures. 'She spins it too. I had a go spinning some last night.'

'How did you get on?' He finished another pressed flower book and stacked it with the ones from earlier.

'I think I'll stick to selling books.'

He smiled. 'Maybe you just need to practice.'

'I'm a member now of the sewing bee and plan to attend the weekly evenings and learn new craft skills.' She held up the embroidery kit. 'Including embroidery.'

'Did someone make that kit?'

'One of the sewing bee members. Quite a few of them have their own craft businesses.'

He nodded, taking this in. 'It's a hive of activity around here.'

Bea smiled at him as he worked diligently creating the pressed flowers. 'It is.'

He got her meaning and smiled back at her.

After pressing the flowers in the books and stacking them neatly, he went back downstairs, having learned what double knitting yarn was. He'd admired the selection of colours in the range of yarn and embroidery threads. Colour was of great interest to Lewis. Bea learned that his favourite colours of paints were in the blue spectrum from the lightest sea foam to cerulean and Prussian blue.

The storm blew against the bookshop's door and the hanging baskets were swinging slightly in the wind. Lewis shrugged his jacket on, an expensive sports style, and zipped the collar up to the high neck.

My goodness, he looked handsome, Bea thought, hoping he couldn't read her thoughts. But he seemed slightly preoccupied, glancing out at the stormy night, and lingering wanting to saying something...

'I had a nice time, Bea.'

'So did I.'

He took a deep breath. 'I wondered...would you like to have dinner with me sometime? Perhaps next week when you've settled into the way of things. An evening when you're not too busy.'

'Yes, I'd like that, Lewis.'

He smiled, relieved that his offer was met with acceptance.

'Okay,' he said, getting ready to face the blast from the sea. 'We'll make a date soon.' He smiled, opened the door and headed out, striding away along the esplanade, home to his cottage.

Bea watched him until he disappeared. The storm was blowing wild, but the strong figure of Lewis walked through it, as if being part of the elements suited him.

She secured the door, thought the hanging baskets could take their chances, and went through to the kitchen and put the kettle on to boil.

While it boiled, she set up her laptop on the writing desk in the lounge, and tapped Lewis' name into a search.

His website popped up and she clicked on it, eager to see his paintings, but the first image to catch her attention was a picture of Lewis, looking handsome yet distant, standing against a backdrop of the sea somewhere in Scotland. When she studied it, she noticed it was along the coast. She recognised the outline of the coast and the islands. So there he was, with those intense blue eyes and sexy hair, unsmiling, gazing out at her. She thought she'd only looked at him for a few moments, but when she heard the kettle click off, she realised she'd been enthralled just gazing at him.

After making a cup of tea, she sat down at the writing desk and flicked through the paintings on his website. Ethel was right. Lewis' artwork was wonderful. A handsome and talented man — and eager to help out in the kitchen with dinner. She smiled to herself thinking of him toasting the cheese on the rumbledethumps like a pro, and serving their dinner by the fire.

The fire had almost burned itself out by the time she'd finished trawling his paintings, admiring his techniques for creating skies that merged beautifully with the sea. Everything about his paintings had an atmosphere to them. Despite Lewis saying he hadn't captured the atmospheric effects of a rainy day, he had, he definitely had. The impression she received from his paintings was one of appreciation of the elements.

The embers in the fire glowed as she closed the laptop and flicked the lamps off to get ready for bed.

His dinner invitation had surprised her, then for a flicker of a second she felt suspicious. His offer seemed genuine, but was there a hint of something else? Did he still have his eye on the bookshop, or to be precise, the cottage? Was she wrong to trust him? Her record of picking trustworthy men wasn't great. Her heart would be broken for sure if she let Lewis into her life. And yet...she wanted to believe that there were decent men out there, men like the postmaster, Tavion and Big Sam.

Tread warily, she warned herself. The bookshop was perfect and she should be happy here with that alone. Lewis could complicate everything. He already had. She'd have dinner with him, but resist taking things further until she was sure of his motives and if her heart was willing to take a chance on love.

CHAPTER EIGHT

Afternoon Tea

Bea ate porridge for breakfast in the cottage kitchen. Gazing out the window, she saw that the storm had battered many of the spring flowers. A few hardy plants perked up in the pale sunlight, but she was thankful she'd picked the flowers the previous day for pressing.

Overnight sales had been great and she'd packed the orders before cooking the porridge. The books were in the trolley ready to be taken along to the post office. It wasn't a day for the courier pick up, but the postmaster stored the parcels ready.

A message popped up on Bea's phone. It was from Ethel. *Did you mention me to Lewis when you were having dinner last night?*

She smiled to herself. Was there anything Ethel didn't know?

Bea replied. *I spoke about your new yarn. Why?*

There's something I need you to see.

I'm on my way.

Bea dropped the parcels off at the post office and then headed to Ethel's cottage. The door was open.

'Come away in, Bea,' Ethel called to her.

'Is there something wrong?' Bea asked breathless from hurrying. But then she noticed Ethel was grinning and pointing to one of the walls in the living room.

Bea looked and saw a painting hanging up. A beautiful seascape. Bea walked up to it, admiring the colours, the texture of the oil paints on the canvas.

Bea read the artist's signature, and gasped. 'Lewis?'

Ethel couldn't stop smiling as she sat on one of her chairs near a spinning wheel, admiring the painting. 'I can't keep it obviously, but I couldn't resist hanging it up to admire it for a wee bit. Isn't it lovely. The way he's captured the froth on the sea and the sweep of the coastline, and all those gorgeous blues — my favourite turquoise and sea blue.' She sighed. 'It makes me feel relaxed just looking at it.'

Bea nodded. It did have that effect, and yet... 'Where did you get it?'

'Lewis dropped it off this morning. He says he wants me to have it — to make amends for blaming me for all the trouble the other night. But it's worth a lot of money, Bea. I don't like to accept it. Unless you know of a reason why I should keep it. Did you mention me to him last night?'

'I told him you admired his paintings and that they were a bit expensive,' Bea summarised the details. 'He was taken aback by your attitude, not holding a grudge against him and praising his art.'

'The painting lights up that wall a treat,' Ethel enthused. 'And it goes well with the colours of my yarn.'

Bea agreed. The shelves were brimming with all the colours of Ethel's yarn and her love of blues was obvious. The painting did blend in well.

'The atmosphere of it makes my heart feel happy and it's very relaxing to look at.' Ethel glanced at the spinning wheels, all filled with yarn of different colours and textures, each one waiting for Ethel to continue spinning the new yarns. 'I'm up to my eyeballs in orders. I need all the calm I can get.'

'Yes, I can see that,' said Bea.

Ethel leaned back and folded her arms as she continued to view the painting. 'I think I'll keep it until the next sewing bee night. The ladies would love to see one of Lewis' paintings for real, up close. None of us have ever done that. Even when he was painting near the esplanade, he never encouraged any of us to stop and have a gander when we were walking past. You could have a peek obviously, but it's different admiring it up close.'

'That's a great idea.' Bea thought the women would appreciate this.

Ethel smiled at her. 'Things seem to be perking up between you and Lewis. Has he asked you out on a date yet? Were you canoodling?'

'No canoodling, but he's invited me to have dinner with him next week.'

'Next week?'

'He's giving me time to reopen the bookshop. We'll have dinner when I'm less busy.'

'Sounds like we've got a budding romance.'

'I wouldn't go as far as that. I'm still a bit wary.'

'Have you decided when you'll open the bookshop?'

'Tomorrow.' Bea sounded determined.

'Good luck to you.'

'I'm anxious thinking about the reopening, so I may as well open up and get on with it. Dive in at the deep end.'

Ethel admired the seascape. 'That's often the best way.'

Bea smiled. 'I'd better get going. I've things to do before Judith picks me up.'

'Enjoy your afternoon tea with the dressmaker.'

'Have you heard anything about why she wants me to visit her?'

'Not a peep, but you can trust her. It won't be anything devious. Listen to what she says, and remember it. Advice from the dressmaker is always valuable.'

'Okay.' Bea started to walk away.

Ethel called after her. 'Don't tell the dressmaker about Lewis giving me the painting. I don't want your visit to be about me. Don't muddy the water with that.'

Bea hesitated.

'Promise me,' Ethel insisted.

'I promise.'

A customer was lingering outside the bookshop as Bea headed back. The young woman was very attractive, fashionably dressed, around thirty, with long dark hair that swished in the morning breeze. She swept it back with a slender and elegant hand and smiled as Bea approached.

'Great, I was hoping you'd be here,' the woman said brightly. 'I saw the closed sign was up, but I'd heard the bookshop had reopened.'

'I'm sorry, but I'm not officially opening until tomorrow.'

The woman's lovely face with its delicate features and dark eyes showed her disappointment. 'Oh, right...'

'Was there a particular book you wanted?' Bea asked, reacting to the customer's deflated sigh.

The woman perked up and pointed to one of the books in the window display. 'That book there. It's my favourite historical romance.'

Bea smiled. 'It's one of my favourites too, that's why I put it in the window.'

The woman lingered, looking hopeful, but didn't push for Bea to sell her the book.

Bea unlocked the door and tucked the trolley behind it. 'Come in.'

The customer stepped inside and gazed around. 'It's a lovely bookshop. It seems the same as the last time I was in here.'

'I've kept it more or less as it was,' Bea explained, switching on the computer to make the sale. 'Are you from around here?'

'No, just visiting again.'

'I hope the weather picks up for you. It was quite a storm last night.'

'You don't sound as if you're local,' the woman commented.

'I'm from Glasgow.'

'A city girl. Far from home.'

'This is my home now.'

Bea lifted the book from the window and popped it in a paper bag.

The woman wandered over to the pressed flower books on the table. 'Are these for sale? I'd like one of them. I saw them advertised on the website.'

Bea saw no reason why she shouldn't include it in the sale. 'Yes. What one would you like? They're all the same price.'

'Do you have one with bluebells in it?'

'No, just the roses and summer selections.' Then she remembered. 'I do have one with bluebells, but it's fresh, the flowers haven't had time to press and dry. You'd need to keep it unopened and weighted down for a few weeks before it was ready.'

The woman sounded enthusiastic. 'I'll take it. I love bluebells. And I'm in no hurry to open it.'

'It's upstairs in the nook. I'll pop up and get it for you.' Bea hurried upstairs, picked up the book Lewis had made with all the lovely bluebells, and ran back down. 'Here you are.'

The woman was delighted. 'Thank you, this is perfect.'

Bea accepted the payment and the sale went through without a hitch. Her first customer was done and dusted. She felt a sense of achievement and relief. This would make it easier when she opened tomorrow. She'd had her first sale.

The customer smiled and clutched the bag with the books as if she'd been given a special treasure. 'Did you press the flowers in the book yourself?' She asked before leaving.

'No, someone else made that one.'

'Can I ask who?' she enquired sweetly.

'His name is Lewis. He's a local artist.'

The woman smiled. 'I've heard of him. He's very handsome, isn't he, Bea?'

The comment jarred Bea, and her senses sparked on alert. The way the woman said her name, the look in her eyes, a spark of jealousy, perhaps resentment.

Bea was so taken aback that she hesitated in replying or questioning the woman.

Carrying the books, the woman walked away. There was a sense of satisfaction in her high–heeled stride.

Bea closed the door and locked it, then hurried over to the till and checked the name on the payment transaction. *Vaila.*

'Her name is Vaila,' Bea told Ethel, phoning her immediately.

'I've never heard of her. From your description, she sounds very attractive.'

'She is. Slender, stylish and sneaky.'

'Don't upset yourself on her account. Snooty troublemakers like her aren't worth it.'

'She said she'd been in the bookshop before, but she's not local.'

'Perhaps a holidaymaker, or from one of the outlying small towns. Remember, this is the only bookshop in the area.'

Bea sighed heavily.

'Make a cuppa and calm down. You've a nice afternoon tea to look forward to. Don't let that wee madam spoil it.'

'You're right, Ethel.'

Bea made a cup of tea and sipped it while sitting in the bookshop, surrounded by the comforting atmosphere of the books. She'd picked up one of her favourites from the classic shelf and started to read the first chapter. Soon, she was lost in a faraway world that soothed her jangled nerves. By the time she'd finished drinking her tea, her equilibrium had been restored.

She put the book back on the shelf, and got on with the business things she wanted to do, including familiarising herself with the system for restocking the books and keeping track of the inventory.

In one drawer of the counter was a selection of small notices to put up on the shop door. These included — closed until Monday, back in five minutes, back in a few days, and late night opening. Ethel had told her that the back in a few days notice indicated Acair's trips to Dundee to visit his girlfriend. He usually left a set of keys with the postmaster in case of any book sales emergencies. It wasn't the first time that the postmaster had opened up the bookshop to let customers buy a special book for someone's birthday or allowed visitors in to buy their holiday reads.

The photograph album caught her attention and she lifted it down from the shelf. The pictures showed the bookshop and local area at different times of the year. She studied photos of the seashore, fields and coastal scenery during warm summer days when bunting stretched along the esplanade and the sea contained all the colours so prevalent in Lewis' painting. In the autumn, the fields appeared to glow like burnished gold, and matched the sunsets where the sky cast the sea in shades of shimmering copper and bronze. The winter scenes showed wild, stormy seas on cold days when the grey skies created an atmosphere of energy and encouraged people to hurry home and snuggle cosy in their cottages before the rain swept along the coast. The snow scenes looked magical, from wintry days when the trees in the forest were frosted to perfection, to the snow covered fields where someone had built a snowman in Tavion's garden.

Having lost a huge slice of time reading books in the shop, Bea realised she had to get herself tidied up. Judith would be here soon.

Judith arrived on time. She wore a woolly cardigan she'd knitted herself, and a blouse and skirt. She was eager to have a look around the bookshop while Bea grabbed her bag.

Judith was reading one of the books when Bea hurried through. She closed the book and sat it back in the window display. 'I'll buy a copy of that book when you open the bookshop tomorrow morning.'

She smiled and admired Bea's outfit, all in shades of grey, from the soft, pale grey jumper embellished with a scattering of silver beads around the neckline that created the effect of a necklace, to the charcoal trousers and classy courts. 'You look a treat.'

Bea smiled at the compliment, but then asked, 'How did you know I was opening tomorrow? Did Ethel tell you?'

Judith hesitated. 'No, Ethel didn't mention it.' Without further explanation, Judith bustled the two of them out to the car. 'Come on, we don't want to be late.'

The car wound its way from the shore, to the fields and then disappeared into the forest. The road was shielded in parts by a canopy of trees, some evergreens, and others covered in spring blossom.

'It's beautiful here,' Bea enthused.

'I love the seashore, and you can glimpse it through the trees.' Judith pointed out the window.

Bea looked and saw the sea shimmering in the afternoon light that streamed through the clouds in the pale grey sky. She felt she'd dressed to match the weather, camouflaged amid the elements.

'But I love the forest,' Judith continued. 'There's something otherworldly about it. I suppose it's from all the fairytale books I used to read when I was a young girl, imagining myself deep in the heart of a bluebell wood with fairies dancing in the glow of fireflies.'

'There's a strong sense of being hidden from the world here in the forest.' Bea sat back in the seat and watched the scenery flit past. The road appeared to wind through a bluebell wood and then double back on itself, before continuing into the forest where the roots of the trees were gnarled across the land, like nature's fingers carved from wood, entwined to keep the forest safe from harm.

There was the glimpse of a cottage here and there, but no hint of people. And it was so wonderfully quiet.

'Do you live in the forest?' said Bea.

'No, I have a house further along the coast. And Tiree lives somewhere nearby. The dressmaker lives on her own in the forest, but I'm there most days, assisting with everything that's needed for her business.'

'Are you joining us for afternoon tea?' said Bea.

'For a wee bitty, but Tiree is busy assisting with the new dress designs for a television historical drama, and I'm helping her organise the fabric. The dressmaker created the outfits for a previous drama and she's been asked to do another one. And she designed dresses, along with Tiree, for Hollywood. The three of us attended the London premiere. It was so exciting.'

'I don't really know anything about the dressmaker, but everyone says her designs are brilliant.'

'They are. She also has some of her own fabrics printed, mainly floral prints, on everything from silk and satin to chiffon and cotton. But at the moment, she's working on the drama costumes.'

'I love historical dramas,' said Bea.

'The television series is based on the popular new novel. There's a copy of it in your bookshop. You've got it in the window. The one with the old fashioned flowers on the cover. Acair ordered copies due to the dressmaker's involvement in the series. The dressmaker loves books.'

Bea smiled. 'I'll definitely read that book now.'

They continued to drive through the forest, and glimpses of sunlight shone through the trees.

'I hope you had a light lunch,' said Judith.

'I skipped it. I was busy reading.'

'You'll have more room for scones, cake and sandwiches.'

'Sounds delicious.' Bea realised she was quite hungry.

'We're almost there,' Judith said, as Bea soaked in the ethereal atmosphere and tranquillity.

By the time they arrived at the traditional, two–storey cottage, Bea was both relaxed and excited as they got out of the car.

Bea stood outside the cottage, breathing in the air that was filled with the scent of flowers and greenery. No hint of the sea. The trees filtered it out, leaving only the floral fragrance in the air.

'Come away in, Bea,' said Judith. 'The dressmaker is looking forward to meeting you.'

Bea followed Judith, but glanced back over her shoulder at the garden amid the forest, feeling the urge to wander there.

'You can have a stroll later,' Judith assured her.

'Judith,' Bea whispered urgently. 'Do you know why I've been invited? Is there anything I should know, or do?'

Before Judith could reply, Thimble came running out of the front door, tail up in welcoming. He wound himself around Bea's ankles, purring, and yet effectively hurrying her inside the cottage.

A table was set in the living room and covered with a white linen tablecloth embroidered with flower motifs at the edges. Cake stands were filled with delicious scones, crustless dainty sandwiches, and slices of cake — Victoria sponge, rich chocolate cake and slices of traditional fruit cake. Fondants and truffles nestled on the stands.

The dressmaker stood beside a wall of fabric that looked as if it was for decorative purposes rather than the working fabric for the dress designs. Each roll was neatly stacked on shelves, colour coordinated, like the dressmaker herself whose sky blue tea dress blended with the pale blue–grey walls, and her light blue eyes were in this calm spectrum. Of retirement age, the dressmaker retained a youthful upright posture. As she walked towards Bea in welcoming, her slender, elegant build moved as easily as the silky fabric of her dress.

She wore her blonde hair in a chignon and minimum makeup on her pale, beautiful face, and extended her hand. 'I'm so pleased you could come, Bea.'

Judith fussed with the seating, edging Bea towards the seat opposite the dressmaker.

Bea smiled. 'Thank you for inviting me.'

Patio doors were closed, but Bea saw that they led on to a lovely garden where a variety of flowers bloomed, unharmed by the storm. The overarching trees in the forest had surely protected everything within the forest from the elements.

Off the living room was the sewing room, a hive of activity with Tiree busy working on the dresses. She popped her head out and waved.

Bea waved back and smiled. 'I hope I'm not interrupting your work.'

'Not at all,' the dressmaker assured her. 'We're always busy. Help yourself to something to eat. You must be hungry.'

'I am,' Bea agreed.

'A busy time getting ready to reopen the bookshop.' The dressmaker's gentle manner reassured her, and yet she felt those pale blue eyes could see right through her. Not in a disconcerting way. It was the strangest feeling, being at ease as a newcomer, genuinely welcome and her situation understood. No prying questions except for one.

'Did you leave anyone you cared about behind in Glasgow, Bea?'

'No. I've no family left since my mother passed years ago. I was barely an adult. I got myself a job working for the finance company and had been there ever since.'

The dressmaker smiled and there was praise in her voice. 'Until you bought the bookshop. What a challenging thing to do, especially being all alone.'

'I hope I've done the right thing,' Bea admitted.

'Oh, you have, Bea. You have.'

Judith poured the tea on a dresser laden with other tasty treats in case what was on offer wasn't to Bea's taste.

'Here you go,' said Judith serving up the tea to Bea and the dressmaker and pouring a cup for herself and Tiree.

Bea took a sip of tea and then helped herself to a dainty cheese and salad sandwich and one of the fluffy scones, filling it with strawberry jam and cream.

Before biting into her food, Bea said to the dressmaker, 'Lewis asked me to thank you for your advice, about painting the snowscapes in winter.'

'Ah, yes, Lewis. He's still hasn't gone back to the isle.' The dressmaker seemed pleased with this. 'Judith told me all about him chasing you down at the shore.'

'I wish now I'd joined in,' Judith admitted, adding a slice of chocolate cake on to her plate.

'So do I,' Tiree piped up from the sewing room.

'It's your own fault for being so well behaved,' the dressmaker teased them.

'Next time I'm having a glass of Ethel's ginger wine,' said Judith.

The dressmaker laughed lightly at this and then said to Bea, 'Don't be fooled, Judith doesn't need any potent concoctions to misbehave.'

Tiree was heard laughing.

'Or you, Tiree,' the dressmaker called to her.

Over afternoon tea, chatter, laughter and gossip was shared between the women, along with a deeper understanding of each other, and new friendships made.

CHAPTER NINE

The Tea Dress

'None of us will have an appetite for our dinner,' the dressmaker said, then bit into a chocolate truffle and sipped her tea. Clearly she didn't give a hoot.

'Shame about that.' Judith helped herself to another salmon sandwich and cream filled meringue.

'Speak for yourselves,' Bea told them. 'I've been burning everything up since I arrived here.' Bea's plate had a second scone with jam and cream and a slice of fruit cake waiting to be enjoyed.

'Oh to be young and fired up on romance,' the dressmaker said with a smile.

Bea looked at her.

The dressmaker smiled. 'What? Don't tell me that Lewis isn't buttering your toast for you.'

Judith guffawed and spluttered at the dressmaker's remark. 'Don't make me drop my salmon sandwich.'

At the mention of salmon, Thimble meowed. He was sitting looking innocent in his basket near the patio doors, but his whiskers were covered in whipped cream. No one knew if cream from one of the meringues was missing, but if it was, the guilty party's whiskers were tipped with it.

'Don't worry,' Judith assured Thimble. 'There's plenty of leftover salmon for your dinner.'

Satisfied that he'd secured his dinner order, Thimble snuggled down and snoozed.

'Come and get your tea and something to eat,' the dressmaker called to Tiree. 'And can you bring the gift bag with you please?'

Tiree emerged from the sewing room, smiling, and carrying a large bag, like a tote bag, and handed it to Bea.

Taken aback, Bea accepted it and peered inside, then glanced in delight at the women.

'Try it on,' the dressmaker told her. 'See if it fits, so we can alter it before you go.'

Bea lifted a beautiful floral print tea dress from the bag. A classic wraparound stitched to perfection and made from a soft cotton fabric with a layer of chiffon. 'A dress?' It was all she could say to being handed the unexpected gift.

'I want you to have it,' the dressmaker told her.

Bea held it up against her. She loved it immediately and couldn't wait to try it on. She hurried into the sewing room and put it on. Being a wraparound, it was an easy fit and the length was ideal.

'Let's have a look,' the dressmaker called to her.

Bea walked out smiling, loving the way the fabric moved when she walked.

'Oh, very nice. It suits you.'

The others agreed with the dressmaker.

'Those court shoes work well with it,' Tiree commented.

'You look lovely, Bea,' said Judith.

Bea's green eyes were wide with delight. 'I didn't expect you to give me a dress.' *Stitched with magic?* The words filtered through her mind, but she never said anything about this to the dressmaker.

'The dressmaker made it specially for you,' Judith told Bea.

Bea smiled at the dressmaker and then ran over and gave her a hug. 'Thank you. I love it.'

The dressmaker fussed and checked that it fitted well, and it did. 'Wear it when you need it,' she told Bea, sounding as if she was imparting advice. Bea made an effort to take this in, remembering what Ethel had told her.

'The bookshop is one of the anchors for this seaside community,' the dressmaker said to Bea. 'It's important that it reopens. Acair did us proud for many years, now it's your turn. I'm glad you're the one to carry the torch. I feel it's in safe hands.'

'I intend to do my best,' Bea promised. 'I've always loved books, and even though I'm new here, I feel welcome, at home, rather than a newcomer.'

'Many of us aren't originally from here, including me,' the dressmaker explained. 'Tiree only arrived fairly recently, as did Mairead at the flower hunter's cottage, and Ethel is originally from Falkirk. But this is your home now.'

As the afternoon light began to fade, it was time for Bea to leave. Tiree continued working in the sewing room, and the dressmaker waved Bea and Judith off at the front door of the cottage.

81

Bea carried the bag containing the tea dress.

'The dressmaker says you're welcome to come back and have a wander around the garden another day,' Judith said to Bea.

Bea smiled, realising this wasn't a one–off visit and she was welcome at the dressmaker's cottage.

Thimble sat on the doorstep, and as they went to get into the car, the dressmaker called to Bea. 'Tell Ethel to keep Lewis' painting.'

Bea glanced back, surprised. She'd kept her promise to Ethel and hadn't mentioned about the painting. But it was the second comment from the dressmaker that made Bea wonder how much the dressmaker knew.

'Don't let a rival interfere with your happiness. Challenge them. Fight for what you want. You've got it in you to do this.'

Bea nodded and exchanged a knowing look with the dressmaker.

Judith drove them back down the twisty–turny route to the seashore, chatting all the way.

'Did Ethel tell you about Lewis's painting?' Bea asked.

'No, Ethel didn't tell me.'

'How did the dressmaker know?'

Judith shrugged and continued driving. 'It's just her way.'

They went on to chat about knitting and sewing.

'I've started knitting a cardigan with Ethel's new yarn,' said Judith. 'One of the pale lavender shades. I thought it would be an ideal colour for the spring.'

'I'm itching to knit something with the yarn Ethel gave me. But I've been so busy.'

Judith smiled and didn't comment.

'I know what you're thinking, Judith. I don't need any special gift like the dressmaker has to sense what you're hinting at.'

Judith laughed. 'Well, you and Lewis have become quiet cosy. If he hadn't been snuggling up in your cottage, helping you of course, you'd have knitted a scarf and matching gloves by now.'

Bea laughed too. 'I keep telling myself not to invite him in, or offer him a cup of tea.'

'A man like him is hard to resist, especially when he's good company and being helpful.'

Bea perked up. 'Things are going to be different once I open the bookshop. I have a schedule planned.'

'I'd keep that schedule flexible. The Lewises of this world can derail a woman's best intentions.'

'Speaking from experience?'

'Nooo. My late husband was down to earth and steady. He loved pottering around in the garden while I did my knitting and sewing. We were content.'

Bea nodded thoughtfully.

'I'm not suggesting that Lewis isn't the settling down type,' Judith continued. 'But I get the impression he's still got a bit of the will–o'–the–wisp in him. For whatever reason. Something in that man needs to be resolved.'

Bea didn't argue. 'I'm determined to cast on some stitches tonight and knit a few rows with that lovely yarn.'

'Let me know if you need any knitting patterns,' Judith offered. 'I have tons ranging from easy–peasy to I wish I'd never started this.'

Bea smiled. 'I'm a mid–range knitter. Scarves are my go–to. I'll tackle a cardigan in stocking stitch, and avoid any fancy cable patterns, but I've never got the hang of knitting neat buttonholes.'

'My favourite is tea cosies. I can knit one up in an evening. Half the community has one of my cosies keeping their teapots warm. There's even one in your kitchen.'

'The yellow and brown stripped tea cosy with the little bees?'

Judith nodded.

'I love it.'

'I knitted the pot holders too. All the quilted items in the cottage were stitched by the sewing bee members. We used to spoil Acair.'

'I guessed that the members had sewn the book fabric quilt.'

'We made it recently. Several of us pieced it together. Hilda is a talented longarm quilter and she machined it into the finished quilt. Acair left it because he said it belonged in the bookshop cottage.'

The car emerged from the forest, and Bea admired the fields and the sea. Bands of pink and amber light shone across the sky as the day began to fade.

'It's a lovely view,' said Judith. 'I enjoy it every time I drive down. We're in for a nice evening. No storm tonight.'

When they arrived back at the bookshop, Bea got out of the car. 'I had a great time, Judith.'

'We all did,' said Judith. 'See you soon, and good luck with the opening tomorrow. I'll be one of your first customers.'

Bea waved Judith off and went into the bookshop. Twilight was descending, but she decided to go for a walk along the shore. She wanted to think about the events of the afternoon, and take a wander along the esplanade.

Leaving a lamp on in the bookshop, she locked the door and started to head in the direction of Ethel's cottage, walking past several cottages on the way.

A sea breeze blew through her hair and she gazed out at the gentle waves washing on to the shore. She breathed deeply, thinking about the great time she'd had in the afternoon, and planned to enjoy a relaxing evening by the fire. In the morning, she'd open the bookshop and begin her new future. Butterflies of excitement fluttered through her.

'Bea!' a man's voice called to her.

She looked back and saw Lewis running towards her.

'Did you have a nice time with the dressmaker?' he said, catching up. He swept his hair back from his brow and smiled at her.

'Yes, the dressmaker gave me a beautiful dress. And I remembered to give her your message.'

'Thanks.' He glanced around. 'Where are you going? I saw Judith drop you off at the shop.'

'Spying on me?' she joked.

'I saw you from my boat. Unintentional spying.'

'I wanted to go for a walk. I haven't had a chance to look around and breathe in the fresh sea air.'

'There's a better way to do that.'

Bea blinked. 'Is there?'

Lewis thumbed back at his boat. 'I was going to head out on my boat. The sea's calm and I've had a hectic day. It's a great way to unwind. I wondered if you'd like to join me.'

'Go sailing?'

'Yes.'

'Tonight? With you?' She wanted to be clear of what he was offering. She'd never been on a boat, any boat, never mind a fancy one like Lewis owned.

He gazed up at the sky. 'It's going to be a long twilight. Last night's storm cleared the air.'

'I've never gone sailing before,' she confessed.

'You'll be quite safe. I won't go far out. We'll just sail along the coastline.'

She found herself nodding, and walked back with him along the shore to his boat.

He held out his hand had helped her on board. His touch sent a tingle through her. Had he felt it too? She was sure he'd reacted to her touch.

'I've got a warm jacket you can put on if you feel cold,' he said. 'I think it's going to be a calm night, but it'll probably be a bit chilly.'

Maybe from your perspective, she thought, but in my world things are heating up.

The boat sailed off from the harbour. Bea stood on the deck gazing out at the sea, feeling as if they were sailing into the twilight's glow. The sea air felt fresh, and blew through her hair. A sense of freedom, of a new life, charged through her.

She glanced back and saw the light shining from the bookshop, and smiled to herself thinking of the relaxing evening by the fire she'd planned. It was true. Men like Lewis could derail a woman's best intentions. Here she was with the will–o'–the–wisp, but perhaps she was becoming more like the woman she'd always wanted to be. A touch of Lewis' unfettered nature was rubbing off on her. Bea's sensible plans to check the bookshop's website was updated and the accounts were in order were cast aside.

For a second she thought she saw the silhouette of a black cat sitting near the bookshop watching her, but when she looked again, the cat had gone.

Lewis watched Bea as he steered the boat out to his intended distance. The warm glow of the setting sun shone on her hair, creating a halo of amber light around it. An angel or a fiery wildcat? He wondered what Bea was. He'd sampled her kindness and generosity, her willingness to trust him and share her dinner with him. He'd also experienced her wrath when he'd overstepped the line and was given a telling off. He decided she was a balanced mix of the two.

Bea waved to him and smiled. She looked so happy. He sighed as he turned the wheel and steered them along the coastline, between the shore and the islands on the far horizon. He knew he was falling in love with her, but it was the one thing he couldn't do until his past was settled.

With the boat steady on its course, Lewis beckoned her to join him.

Looking like she was having fun, Bea walked towards him, but a small wave caused the boat to tilt slightly. She was unused to adjusting her balance at sea and was flung against Lewis.

Lewis caught her in his arms, and she felt the strong muscles on his chest beneath her fingers.

'Steady there, sailor,' he told her, smiling.

Nothing in her felt steady, standing there in Lewis' arms, so close she could see the flecks of sea green amid the blue of his eyes and breathe in the mild but expensive scent of his cologne.

His hands held her for a moment longer than necessary, lingering as he gazed at her. She thought he was going to lean down and kiss her.

He suddenly blinked out of the moment and released her, smiling awkwardly, and brushed his hair back from his brow in that sexy gesture, sending her heart racing even more. Neither of them said, but they both knew they'd almost given in to their feelings, but she was glad that he'd resisted for she couldn't have done so if he'd pressed those firm lips on hers.

'Until you get your sea legs, would you care to try your hand at steering?'

'You're trusting me to keep us on course?'

'Unless you'd rather not.'

Feigning bravado she straightened to her full height, but was still gazing up at him. 'Show me the ropes, but be prepared for an impromptu trip to the islands.'

He laughed. 'Come on then, landlubber, let's see if you have the potential to handle a boat.'

Bea smiled to herself. She barely had the strength to handle her feelings for him, let alone steer the boat. They'd be adrift at sea soon she mused, taking charge of the ship's wheel, a small wheel, inside the cabin.

Lewis stood behind her, his arms reaching over her shoulders, guiding her hands expertly. Again the touch of his hands on hers sent her heart thundering, but she was determined to keep the boat steady, even if she was feeling all at sea.

Lights from the cottages and farmhouses shone along the coast as the twilight deepened to night.

Lewis finally took control again and steered the boat back towards the harbour.

'That was fun,' Bea said, and then looked around the cabin. Everything was stylish, clean and organised. There was a bunk bed for sleeping, but it didn't look like it had been slept in for a while. Everything was neatly folded.

'I prefer sleeping at the cottage,' he said, reading her well.

'It still looks comfy and spacious with room enough for two,' she remarked, then quickly clarified. 'Not that I'm hinting that I want to go to bed. I'm not sleepy.'

Lewis smirked as she dug herself deeper.

'Nor am I suggesting anything else,' she said, sounding flustered.

Squirming for embarrassing herself, she went over to the small kitchen where the pots and pans gleamed, and hung up alongside every utensil she could name.

'You have more utensils in your cabin kitchen than I have at the cottage.' Everything was thoroughly cleaned, and she wondered if he ever used half of them.

'I like a well–kitted out kitchen,' he explained, sounding as if he grudged admitting it.

Sensing he didn't want to elaborate on his kitchen accoutrements, she gazed out at the view. The light in the bookshop was her compass to where they were, as Lewis sailed the boat smoothly into the harbour and tied the boat to one of the cleats on the dock.

'Thank you for inviting me, Lewis. That was incredible.'

'I'm glad you took a chance to come sailing with me, especially for someone without any experience. Sailing experience,' he added.

'A few more trips and I'll be navigating the high seas,' she said lightly. 'But I'm not hinting for you to invite me out on your boat again.'

'You've been doing a lot of not hinting about a few things this evening.' He smiled warmly.

'I have, haven't I?'

He nodded and continued smiling at her.

'Okay, I'd better get going.'

Lewis jumped off the boat and held his hand out to steady her as she stepped off. He held her hand and wouldn't let go until he'd said to her, 'I wish you all the luck with the bookshop opening.'

'Thank you, Lewis.'

For a moment she thought he would kiss her goodnight, but the moment was gone as a breeze blew between them, a sudden cold gust from the sea.

It was her turn to sweep her hair back from her face as the wind whipped through it.

Although there was no awkwardness, there was a hesitation from both of them, as if they were reluctant to bring their evening to a close.

Taking the first steps to leave, Bea smiled and walked away towards the bookshop. When she was almost there she looked back and saw that Lewis was still standing there where she'd left him. The expression on his face disconcerted her. A soulful look as if he'd let her go but deep down didn't want to.

She waved and he waved back to her, then she went inside the shop. By the time she'd locked the door and looked out the window, Lewis had gone and the lights were switched off in the boat.

The wind picked up pace and swept along the esplanade, and a pang of loneliness hit her. Then she took a deep breath and viewed the welcoming shelves filled with books, and realised that as long as she was safely tucked amid the books she was never truly alone.

The bag containing the tea dress sat on the counter where she'd left it. She picked it up and went through to the bedroom and hung it up on the outside of the wardrobe to admire it. She'd worn dresses to parties and various company events, but no amount of sequins or sparkle could outshine this tea dress designed by the dressmaker. It was priceless. She ran her hands down the lovely fabric and held the hem out, imagining wearing it for a special occasion. Whatever that would be. The stitching was perfect and the layer of chiffon had been expertly sewn into the design.

She stepped back to admire it. Yes, it was perfect. If there was magic sewn into it, that was a lovely notion, but she wasn't inclined to believe in fairytales.

As she walked out of the bedroom into the living room to light the fire, a noise sounded from the bookshop.

Bea hurried through. She'd definitely locked the door.

In the shadowed glow of the lamp, she peered around. No one was there. Outside the wind swirled past, and she relaxed. She'd have to get accustomed to the noises in the bookshop, especially as most of it was made from wood and it was surely affected by the weather.

But then she noticed that one of the books had tumbled down and was lying on the floor near the window display. She picked it up and noticed it was the book Judith said she'd wanted. The novel that the television drama series was based on.

She flicked on the computer and checked the stock. It was the last one of that title. Instead of putting it in the window, Bea tucked it under the counter, in safe keeping for Judith in case she wanted it.

She checked the orders and emails. There was an email an hour ago from Aurora with an attachment. She opened it and read the editorial Aurora had written for the feature. It was flattering, and interesting, and the photographs to go with it were wonderful. As promised, Lewis was credited for creating some of the pressed flower books and there was a link to his website.

Bea quickly typed a reply to Aurora as she'd requested a fast reply due to the deadline.

The feature is brilliant! I wouldn't change a word of it. Thank you for writing this and including me in your magazine.

She pressed the send button and hoped Aurora received it in time.

I'm happy you're pleased, Bea. Your bookshop article is one of the magazine's main features this issue. I'll email a link when it's published. It goes live at midnight this evening.

Bea smiled. Things were starting to feel exciting. Within hours the feature would be read online in the magazine. Perfect timing for the opening of the bookshop in the morning.

CHAPTER TEN

Embroidery and Yarn

Rain pattered on the cottage windows, but Bea sat cosy by the fire enjoying her savoury omelette supper. The afternoon tea had kept her fuelled up long into the evening, but as the night wore on and she'd sorted everything for the opening in the morning, she made a tasty omelette with cherry tomatoes, peppers, spring onions and Scottish cheese.

She was too excited to settle down and go to bed earlier, so she made supper and snuggled by the fire. The lamps in the living room added to the warmth, and it was soothing listening to the rain hitting off the windows.

Her laptop was set up on the writing desk, and as midnight approached, she heard the ping of an email.

Aurora was working late and sent her a link to the latest issue of the magazine. Bea sat at the desk and read through the features, cheering to herself when she saw that the bookshop feature was on the front page. The bookshop looked great in the photos.

Ethel's new collection of yarn was another main feature. The colours of the yarn were gorgeous, and it included free knitting patterns for a scarf and wrist warmers, cardigan and a tea cosy. The patterns tempted Bea, and she dug out the yarn from her knitting bag, wondering if she should consider knitting the scarf.

The magazine also had free embroidery patterns for various flowers including bluebells and pansies. Bea imagined these would be popular. Using the embroidery kit Aurora gave her was certainly on her to–do list.

There were recipes in the magazine for hearty soups and delicious cakes, and she definitely intended making the Scottish tablet and tattie scones. The red lentil soup recipe put her in the notion to cook up a pot of it, and she had to close the feature as it was making her hungry again and it was too late at night to be rattling around in the kitchen making soup and baking cakes.

A message came through on her phone from Ethel.
Are you still up?

Yes, have you seen the features in the magazine?
That's what I was pinging you for. The bookshop looks great.
I love it. Love your yarn feature too. Think I'll knit a scarf.
I see that Lewis got a mention.
He did. He was happy to be included.
He's certainly become Mr. Friendly these days. Your influence, Bea.
The dressmaker says you should keep Lewis' painting. I didn't blab.
Great. I'll keep it. Did you enjoy your afternoon tea with the dressmaker?
She gave me a dress!
Wow!
I know! I'll tell you all about it tomorrow.
Get some sleep. Exciting day ahead. I'll be one of your first customers.
See you in the morning. Lots of gossip to tell.

Bea went to finish the messaging, but there was a final one from Ethel.

I didn't know you could sail a boat. There's no end to your talents, Bea!

Bea laughed. Yes, there was definitely a lot of gossip to chatter about in the morning.

Climbing into bed, Bea snuggled under the quilt and watched the rain hit off the window. She thought about her visit to the dressmaker's cottage, the dress that was now hanging on her wardrobe, the feature in the magazine — and Lewis. It would be so easy to fall for him. She kept picturing those blue eyes of his, the way he looked at her, and almost kissed her...

Listening to the rain, and thinking about sailing with Lewis, she fell asleep and slept sound until the morning.

Sunlight shone through the front window of the bookshop. It was a bright spring day, and Bea was excited to open the bookshop. She'd been up early, had cereal and fresh fruit for breakfast, and was on her second cup of tea.

She wore a pale yellow blouse and dark trousers, and tied her hair back in a tidy ponytail. The computer on the counter was fired up, ready to deal with customer orders, as was Bea.

The opening hours were ten in the morning until four in the afternoon, five days a week, closed Sunday and Monday. These were the shop's opening times in the past.

The excitement built inside her as she went over to the door, unlocked it and flipped the closed sign to open. Phew! Here we go, she thought, wondering if she'd be busy or quiet, run off her feet or would have time to read a chapter or two of the book she was currently enjoying.

Barely a minute later, she heard the sound of cheerful voices, and peeked out the door to see several of the sewing bee members, led by Ethel, loaded with two shopping bags, heading for the shop. Hilda was carrying a cake box, Aurora held up a bottle of bubbly and waved to Bea, and the smiles and laughter continued until they were outside the bookshop clapping and cheering her official opening.

The postmaster came hurrying along, having seen them go by the post office. Ethel thrust her phone at him. 'Take a photo of us outside the bookshop. Make sure you get everyone in, including Ione.' She waved Ione to stand closer and to stop peering in the window.

Being swept along in the hustle and bustle, Bea let herself be positioned between Ethel and Aurora, back by Hilda, Tiree and Ione.

'Wait for me,' Judith shouted, scurrying from her car to join them. 'My clock was barmy this morning.'

The only thing that was barmy, Bea thought, was the whole situation. A gaggle of women, friends galore, backing her to the hilt, and insisting they set up a buffet in her kitchen.

'Leave everything to us, Bea,' Ethel told her, adjusting her position as the postmaster tried to get everyone into the picture. 'You concentrate on dealing with the customers. We'll get the buffet set up.'

'Smile!' the postmaster shouted to them. He clicked several pictures, then everyone rearranged themselves, and other members joined them, until there was a throng outside.

The tall figures of Tavion and Big Sam anchored the edges of the small crowd, and Bea found herself glancing at Lewis' boat, wondering if he was there and would run over to join them. But there was no sign of him. She was surprised at the strength of her disappointment.

A farmer passing by had the phone thrust at him by the postmaster. 'Take a photo with me it, will you?'

'Happy to oblige,' the farmer said.

The postmaster wangled his way in until he was standing beside Ethel. He put his arm around her shoulder and pulled her close. She made no move to extricate herself, and her smile lit up all the brighter for being coupled with the postmaster.

Ethel was handed her phone by the farmer and he continued on his way. She checked the pictures. 'These look great, Bea!'

Bea took a peek and nodded. She almost shed a happy tear seeing herself surrounded with all the genuinely friendly faces, something that a lifetime of living in the city had never come close to.

'I'll add these to the photo album in the bookshop,' Bea said, thinking that years from now she'd look back and remember how happy they all were. Simple pleasures and good times were worth all the effort of coming here.

Photos taken, they headed into the shop. Bea was installed behind the counter and told not to lift a finger unless to sell a book while the ladies busied themselves in the kitchen.

'I didn't expect to have a special launch,' said Bea, delighted.

'It was a spur of the moment thing this morning,' Ethel confessed. 'We'd promised ourselves we weren't going to interfere, and then we all thought — let's do it!'

Ione plopped two large jars full of sweets down at the side of the counter. 'I brought these to keep your customers sweet.' She smiled and then hurried through to the kitchen.

Bea looked at the chocolate caramels and strawberry creams. Her hands were in the jar helping herself and popping one in her mouth as she finished her cup of tea.

'I'll make you a fresh, hot cup of tea,' Hilda said to Bea. 'Just after I cut this cake.' In the cake box was a big Dundee cake, as deep as the cake box itself, glistening with glazed dried fruit, almonds and glacé cherries.

The postmaster grinned and handed Bea a large book he intended to buy. A non–fiction hardback about Scottish trains. 'I'm your first official customer this morning. I've had my eye on this book since Christmas, then everything went to poppycocks and I never got around to buying it.'

Bea took charge of the sale, and then he headed back to the post office with his book, and chewing on a chocolate caramel.

Ione had her hands full with two craft books — one with new soft toy patterns and the other with ideas for weddings. She swithered which one to buy.

Big Sam reached over and lifted both books. 'My treat, Ione.' He put them on the counter. 'I'll take both of these.'

Ione kissed him as he handed the books to her.

One after the other, Bea's friends and acquaintances purchased one or two books. She knew this wouldn't be a regular occurrence, but she was grateful for their back–up for her first day's sales.

Tavion bought a men's adventure novel and a copy of Fintry the flower hunter's new non–fiction book. 'I enjoy reading about the backgrounds of flowers,' he told Bea, and then took the books away with him.

Judith looked disappointed as she searched for the copy of the book she'd planned to buy. 'I guess someone snapped it up,' she said to Bea.

Bea reached under the counter and produced the book. 'I put it aside for you, just in case.'

Judith perked up. 'Brilliant! I'd told the dressmaker I was going to buy it, and she was interested in having a read at it too. And she asked me to buy these for her.' Judith handed Bea a short list. 'She said she'd checked that they were available on your website.'

Bea confirmed she had every book on the list, proceeded to pick them from the shelves, put them in a sturdy paper bag and gave them to Judith. 'Thank the dressmaker for her support.'

'I'll do that,' said Judith.

'Here you go, Bea. A nice fresh cuppa.' Hilda placed the tea behind the counter. 'Would you like me to put a slice of Dundee cake aside for you for later?'

'I would, Hilda. Thanks.'

'Has Lewis been in yet?' Hilda asked her.

'No,' Bea replied, making no assumptions or excuses for him.

'Maybe he's waiting until later,' Hilda suggested, and then glanced at the craft books 'If you have any books on quilting, I'll take one of those.'

From the latest thrillers and romance novels, and classic favourites to the current releases, the fiction book sales along with the non–fiction titles, from craft to cookery books, Bea did a roaring trade on her opening day. The buffet kept everyone fed and there was gossip and chatter aplenty. Sewing bee members came and went, bringing more cakes and scones, along with their cheery laughter. The local people came out in support of the bookshop, and Bea met people that were to become regular customers. The bookshop's sales soared.

Winding down in the afternoon, she finally got a chance to chat properly to Ethel. 'My new dress is hanging on my wardrobe. Take a peek if you want.'

Ethel nodded, and was accompanied by several of the ladies as they went through to see what the dressmaker had sewn for her.

The sound of their appreciation filtered through to the bookshop.

Ethel hurried back to Bea. 'That's a beautiful dress.'

'I didn't expect her to give me a dress. Judith said the dressmaker made it specially for me.'

'There's usually a reason for something so specific as this. A particular reason why you need the dress.'

Bea frowned. 'What do you suppose it's for?'

Ethel shrugged. 'Did she advise on anything?'

Bea recounted the conversation. 'She said I should wear the dress when I needed it.'

Ethel looked thoughtful. 'Anything else?'

'She told me not to let a rival interfere with my happiness. To challenge them. To fight for what I wanted. She said I had it in me to do that. I was leaving at the time and didn't get a chance to ask her to elaborate, and yet...I felt I would understand when I needed it. It was the strangest feeling.'

'I know what you mean,' said Ethel.

'She hinted about a romance between Lewis and me—'

'Is anyone serving in the shop?' a snippy voice interrupted, piping up from behind one of the bookshelves.

'That's her,' Bea whispered to Ethel.

'Vaila?' Ethel whispered back.

Bea nodded and exchanged a look with Ethel. Had Vaila been eavesdropping on their conversation?

'Yes,' Bea said brightly, going over to assist her. 'Can I help you?'

Unamused dark eyes stared at Bea. 'I'm looking for a copy of the flower hunter's new book.'

'I sold the last copy, but I can order it in for you,' Bea offered.

'No thank you. I can order it quicker myself.'

There was a lull in the laughter as the sewing bee ladies sensed Vaila's disdainful tone.

Unaware of the tense atmosphere in the bookshop, Big Sam came in all smiles and went right up to Bea. 'Do you have any books on dance etiquette for bridegrooms?'

'I'll check, but I don't think I have.' Bea looked through the listings on the computer.

'We're getting married outdoors on the shore,' he explained. 'That's where we met, and we want to exchange our vows there. Then we're having a reception party in a marquee. Tavion's offered to help set it up on one of his fields. Ione wants everything on video so she can watch it later, and keep it. She's asked me not to act like an eejit for our first dance as a couple. I'm used to burling my kilt, but I want to do things properly.'

Bea sighed. 'I don't have any books like that. But I'd be happy to give you a few tips.'

Big Sam brightened. 'Would you? That would be great. I've never been to any fancy wedding dance parties, just the usual shindigs.'

'I've been to plenty in the city,' Bea told him. 'First dances are easy to learn.'

'Excuse me,' Vaila cut–in. 'I hadn't finished being served.'

Big Sam stepped back immediately. 'Sorry, lass, I didn't know.' He smiled pleasantly and gave her room at the counter.

'And I'm not your lass,' Vaila told him.

Bea glanced at Ethel and Hilda. Some of the other ladies peered in from the kitchen as the atmosphere bubbled with undercurrents of anger, mainly from Vaila.

Big Sam kept his mouth buttoned, not wanting to offend Vaila any further.

Thinking she had them on the ropes, Vaila continued to snipe at Big Sam. 'A word of advice, if you come into a bookshop looking for something specific, try to know what the title of the book is.' Then she added, 'But I can read books. Can you?'

A gasp sounded in the shop as several of the women were shocked at the insult.

Ethel blinked. Had she heard right? She glanced at Hilda who shook her head, indicating it wasn't their place to cause trouble in Bea's shop.

Bea stepped in to defend Big Sam. She looked straight at Vaila. 'Not only can Big Sam read books, he can bind them too. Can you?'

Vaila hesitated, sensing that Bea wasn't the easy target she'd assumed she was. 'This is a pathetic little bookshop. I won't be setting foot in here again.' She started to walk towards the door.

Bea opened the door for her. 'No, indeed you won't.'

Effectively being shown the door, Vaila sneered at Bea on her way out. 'Lewis doesn't love you. He loves me. We're getting married in the summer.'

Bea was floored by the comment, but stood firm, determined not to let Vaila see that her barbed remark hit its intended target — her heart. Lewis was marrying Vaila? Her mind buzzed with the realisation.

'Lewis just wants the bookshop,' Vaila stabbed the verbal dagger in deeper. 'If you thought anything else, you're easily fooled.'

Bea closed the door and watched Vaila strut away towards Lewis' boat.

Several voices of the women chattered, shocked and complaining about Vaila.

'*What a little madam.*'

'*She's got a nerve on her.*'

'*Who does she think she is?*'

'*Is Bea okay?*'

'*She's looking a bit pale.*'

'*No wonder.*'

'*Lewis had us all fooled.*'

The chatter faded into the background, circling around Bea, but not settling. Bea watched Vaila step on to Lewis' boat as if she owned it, and disappeared from view. '*Lewis doesn't love you. We're getting married. He just wants the bookshop.*' The words weighed a ton, pinning her to the spot as she continued to stare out at Lewis' boat. Then she saw Lewis hurrying along the esplanade. He was carrying a picnic basket and didn't even glance at the bookshop.

He jumped on to his boat and joined Vaila below deck. Bea felt her world tilt, as everything she believed about Lewis was cast adrift.

As the chatter continued, one voice brought it to a close. 'She's a liar!' Big Sam said, making himself heard above the rabble.

They all paused and looked at him.

'I'm telling you, that wee bessom is a liar,' Big Sam insisted.

Ethel frowned. 'Why would she lie about a thing like that? She says she's marrying Lewis in the summer.'

Big Sam shook his head. 'She's a troublemaker. She got called out and met her match when Bea stuck up for me.' He looked at Bea. 'Thank you. I didn't want to say anything. If there's one thing I know, it's never to argue with a lass when she's got a toot on.'

'You really think she was lying about getting married?' said Bea.

He nodded firmly. 'I can always tell when a lassie is telling fibs.' He shook his head in dismay. 'She's a snippy wee troublemaker.'

'Who's a troublemaker?' Iona asked, walking in breezily with a small posy of flowers she'd picked from Bea's garden. She'd asked if she could try pressing them in the books upstairs in the nook.

Everyone paused and looked at Big Sam to do the explaining.

It took a slice of cake, two strawberry creams and a cup of tea to calm Ione down. Big Sam fished the bubbles out of her teacup. Ione didn't like bubbles. He put a strong and reassuring arm around her bristling shoulders.

'Don't upset yourself, Ione,' Big Sam said calmly. 'She's not worth it.'

Ione sipped her tea and sighed. 'If only I hadn't picked those extra pansies. I'd have been here and stuck these sprigs up her snooty nose.' Ione huffed. 'Insinuating you're as thick as mince and can't read books! You're a highly skilled bookbinder.'

'Bea showed her the door,' Big Sam reminded Ione. 'Vaila won't be back.'

'Are you okay, Bea?' Ethel asked gently. Obviously she wasn't okay.

Bea imagined she looked as drained as she felt. 'I'll be okay. I'm just a bit deflated. I trusted Lewis. I was warned to be careful but...'

Hilda came through with a cup of tea for her. 'Here you go. Get a wee sip of this.'

Bea accepted it gladly, cupping her hands around it for warmth. It was cosy in the bookshop, but the shock had chilled her to the bone.

'We'll help you close up the shop and pack the orders,' said Aurora. Then she nodded to the ladies, and they all swiftly began tidying things up. Aurora took charge of the computer, marking books that were now out of stock and needed to be reordered.

Bea drank her tea and then stood up and began to work alongside them. She'd taken a hit, but then there were days at work in the city when she suffered a few swipes in one day.

'Thank you all for helping and making the opening a success,' Bea said, tidying one of the shelves and adding other books to the window display where it had been almost emptied of popular titles. 'It was a success,' she emphasised, determined not to let Vaila's interlude spoil what had otherwise been a great day. 'I refuse to let Vaila ruin it. That's what she wanted, and I won't give her that.'

A triumphant cheer rose up from all corners of the bookshop and the kitchen where plates were being cleaned and dishes put away. Everything was left tidy.

Bea was given more warm hugs than she'd had in a year, possibly two years, as they all got ready to leave.

Ethel spoke quietly to Bea. 'Do you want me to stay for a wee while and keep you company? Stop you being on your own and dwelling on things?'

Usually, Bea would've refused the kind offer, but as the twilight descended over the sea, she gazed out the window and then nodded.

Ethel shrugged her coat off, and seeing this the others, one by one, did the same, until they were all ready to make dinner in the cottage.

Aurora grabbed her purse. 'I'll pop along to the grocers before it shuts and get us a big bag of potatoes and turnip. We can have a large pot of thump and whatever else we fancy.'

Judith had left earlier but was now back and eager to help. 'I'll go with you, Aurora.'

Hilda grabbed a masher from the kitchen and wielded it. 'I'll mash the tatties and turnip. I'll get my wind out, picturing it pounding on that troublemaker's bahookie.'

Seeing Hilda standing in the doorway, armed with a tattie masher, made Bea laugh. Soon, others were laughing, and the air cleared of the heavy feeling that Vaila had created.

Big Sam had found a fancy apron in the kitchen cupboard. He'd tied it around his waist and was now dancing up and down the living room, demonstrating how much he was capable of embarrassing Ione at the wedding.

'Bea's going to teach me proper etiquette for our first dance,' he shouted to Ione as he shimmied past her. 'How do you like these moves, eh?' He waggled his apron and just missed being swiped by Ethel's oven mitt.

As laughter filled the cottage and the bookshop, Bea turned her back on the view of Lewis's boat. The lights shone from inside the cabin. But despite having been hurt, she knew she was far better off with these warm–hearted people, laughing away their troubles while making a hearty dinner that they all sat down and shared.

CHAPTER ELEVEN

The Bookshop

Bea locked the bookshop door after waving goodnight to her guests. A light still shone in Lewis' boat, and she tried not to think of him being there with Vaila.

In the morning she planned to get on with her business.

Flicking the lights off, she went through to her bedroom and hung her new dress inside the wardrobe.

The night was so quiet, no sound of the wind blowing in from the sea, or rain.

Snuggling under the duvet, she peered out the window at the calm night, and then tried to go to sleep without dwelling on Lewis.

Bea took a pile of book orders to the post office. It was another bright spring morning. On the way back she bought fresh bread, milk and other items from the grocery shop, put them in the trolley and walked back to the bookshop.

The bookshop's window display now had a new selection of books, and she'd refreshed the vases of flowers, adding pansies from the cottage garden. It looked pretty, she thought, trying to think about the shop and not look over at Lewis' boat. But it was the reflection in the window, a figure standing beside the boat, watching her, that made Bea glance over. And there was Vaila, stylishly dressed, flicking her long hair, staring at Bea.

For a moment, they stared at each other. Vaila had a look of triumph, knowing she'd sunk Bea's hopes of romance with Lewis.

Bea's heart ached when she saw Lewis emerge from the boat's cabin and join Vaila. He hadn't noticed Bea. He was too busy talking to Vaila.

Whatever he was saying made Vaila gaze up at him and smile. When he'd finished, she stood on her tiptoes, kissed him on the lips, and then stared over at Bea with a satisfied smirk.

Bea unlocked the door and went inside the bookshop, shielding herself from seeing any further display from Vaila. She was sure

Lewis hadn't even noticed her as his full attention was on his girlfriend.

Unwilling to watch any further antics from the pair of them, Bea went through to the kitchen and unpacked the groceries. While the kettle boiled she made toast and strawberry jam. Something sweet to take away the bitter aftertaste of seeing Lewis with Vaila.

Finishing her toast, she topped her tea up and carried it through to the bookshop to get on with her work. For a few minutes she looked at the computer screen, viewing the book lists, and then was tempted to peek across at Lewis' boat.

She blinked. The boat had gone. Far in the distance she saw it cut through the waves, heading towards the islands.

She could've wept, but she didn't. Stay strong, she bolstered herself. Fight for what you want. Right now she wanted to make a success of her bookshop. That's what she'd set out to do. Now here she was. Determined to do what she'd always dreamed of, she began reordering books that were out of stock having been sold at the successful opening day. Her fingers flew across the keys, calculating costs, updating the website, ensuring the accounts were balanced and the finances in order. This was what she was good at, and if ever there was a time to put her talent to use, it was now.

Ethel dropped by with fresh baked scones. 'Doing okay, Bea?'

'I'm pushing on with my work, but I'll put the kettle on for tea.'

'I don't want to interrupt.'

'You're not.' Then she sighed and told Ethel what had happened.

Ethel gasped. 'Vaila kissed Lewis so you would see them at it?'

'She did.'

'What did he do?'

Bea shrugged. 'I looked away. I'd seen enough.'

'I noticed his boat has gone.'

Bea nodded. 'I saw it in the distance, heading towards the islands.'

Ethel took out her phone. 'I'll phone Hilda's sister, Jessie. We'll find out where he's gone and what he's up to.'

Bea wasn't sure. 'I don't want to be dwelling on Lewis. He's clearly been lying to me.'

'Ione phoned me. She says Big Sam is certain Vaila's a blether.'

'Lewis knew I was opening the bookshop and he didn't come over. After taking me out on his boat and...well, giving me the impression that things were progressing between us. He didn't even turn up. It's so blatant that he's cast me aside. Not that we were ever together...'

'Lewis has always kept himself to himself — until you arrived. Then he seemed to be happier. Something in his past keeps cropping up, so let me ask Jessie if she knows anything.'

Bea made the tea, put jam and cream on the scones, and listened while Ethel phoned Jessie.

'Find out if Lewis sailed his boat to one of the islands. Find out anything you can. He's been leading Bea on, and I think we deserve to know what he's up to. Okay, Jessie, thanks.'

Bea sipped her tea.

'Jessie says she'll ask around and phone back soon. She agrees with us that his behaviour is unacceptable.'

After tea, scones and a chat, Ethel left to get on with her work, and Bea was quite busy with customers. New faces ventured into the bookshop to browse and buy.

Book orders had perked up online, with notes from some customers mentioning they'd seen the feature in the magazine, and wanted to buy the pressed flower books along with other titles.

Bea emailed Aurora to tell her the response to the feature was great.

As the day wore on Bea found herself glancing out the window, watching to see when Lewis' boat would be back. Despite chiding herself for this, she couldn't help it.

She closed the bookshop at four o'clock, and eased off the tension in her shoulders. The afternoons seemed to be getting longer as spring brightened the sky and refreshed everything.

Ethel chapped on the door and peeked in at her.

Bea welcomed her in.

'Jessie phoned with news,' Ethel said, hurrying inside. 'There's been no sign of Lewis' boat arriving at any of the islands.'

'So he was just having a day sailing along the coast with her,' she said, picturing Lewis dropping anchor offshore, and the two of them relaxing on the deck enjoying a picnic. Would he wrap his arms around Vaila and let her steer the boat?

'Jessie got some background gossip on Vaila. Apparently, her parents are well off and she lives with them on the same isle that Lewis is from. The two sets of parents from their families have been friends for years. There's talk that Lewis and Vaila will get married this summer.'

'Vaila was telling the truth,' Bea said, her hopes sinking.

'That's the strange thing. No one that Jessie spoke to knows Lewis and Vaila as a couple. They've never seen them out together or at parties.'

The sinking halted, buoyed by this shred of hope.

'I'll keep my ears open and let you know if I hear anything else,' said Ethel. She buttoned up her cardigan, ready to leave. 'What are you up to this evening? I hope you find time to relax.'

'Big Sam is coming over for his first lesson.' Bea smiled. 'So that's my evening sorted.'

Ethel laughed and stepped outside the shop.

Aurora came hurrying towards them. 'Ione has a dress emergency. It's all hands on deck at her house tonight to help sew the beading on her wedding dress. She needs to get it finished so she can make a start on her bouquet and other plans for the wedding. I said I'd round up some of the ladies.'

'I'll help her,' Ethel offered.

'Brilliant,' said Aurora, and then looked at Bea.

'I'm teaching etiquette to Ione's other half this evening,' Bea told Aurora.

'Good luck with that.'

They all laughed.

'I've been taking pictures of Ione making her dress,' Aurora explained. 'I'm including it as a main feature in next month's issue of the magazine, after the wedding. It's a beautiful dress. Wedding and bridal features are always popular for spring issues.' She took a deep breath. 'And that's what I wanted to talk to you about, Bea. With the interest shown in the bookshop feature, I'd like to make you a regular part of the magazine. I have a scrapbooking article for the next issue, and maybe we could do another bookshop feature with different pressed flowers and book reviews.'

Bee nodded, eager to participate.

'The dressmaker's feature will highlight the dresses and costumes she's designing for the new television historical drama series,' Aurora enthused. 'It would be brilliant if you could review the novel it's based on.'

'I'd love to,' said Bea.

'We'll chat soon,' Aurora promised. 'I've lots of ideas. And for you too, Ethel.'

As Bea waved them off, she looked over at the harbour. There was no sign of Lewis' boat. She guessed he was making a day and an evening of it sailing with Vaila. Closing the door and locking it, she went through to prepare her dinner, a roast vegetable pizza topped with a lavish selection of tasty vegetables, before Big Sam arrived.

An eager fist pounded on the bookshop door.

Bea smiled to herself and went through from the kitchen to let Big Sam in.

'I'm here to pester you,' he joked. 'What I mean is, to take you up on your kind offer to teach me the etiquette of a proper first dance.'

'I've cleared a space in the living room.' She led him through.

'I'm a bit early, but I've been banned for the night from seeing Ione or the wedding dress. Whenever I've loaded the dress into the back of the car to drive Ione to the sewing bee nights, I've had to do it with my eyes shut.' He demonstrated, closing his eyes and scrambling around.

'Steady there,' Bea said, calming his enthusiasm before he scorched his kilt on the fire.

He smiled at her. 'I don't know anything about wedding dresses, but this is supposed to be a fairytale masterpiece. I'm gearing up to stop myself from greetin' when I see her walking down the aisle. I'm one lucky man.'

Bea thought Ione was lucky too. They were a well–matched couple.

He rubbed his hands together. 'I wore one of my older kilts so that I can experience the swish of the fabric when I'm learning the dancing.'

Bea kicked her shoes off for ease of dancing on the carpet, and it made her equal in height to the petite Ione.

Big Sam measured the height difference with his hand. 'Yes, that's about right,' he said smiling.

There was a lot of laughter as Bea explained a few rules before teaching him the steps of a classic first dance.

He raised a hand and stopped her before she could continue. 'There's something I need to get off my chest. I was warned not to open my mouth, but I need to tell you this.'

'Okay. I won't tell that you told me.'

He was unperturbed. 'Ione and the other women will find out anyway. I'm no use at keeping secrets like this.'

Bea nodded for him to go ahead.

'It's about Vaila.'

The mention of her name jarred Bea, but she wanted to hear what he had to say.

'Vaila wasn't wearing an engagement ring.'

Bea blinked. 'I didn't notice.'

The silversmith in him noticed jewellery. 'Silver rings are something I make a lot of. It's a habit that I look at people's hands to see what's fashionable. Vaila wasn't wearing an engagement ring, but she had two other rings on her fingers, both on her right hand. That means she's a woman who likes wearing rings. With a summer wedding in the not too distant future, I have to wonder why she's not wearing a dazzler on her engagement finger. I think she's the type to flaunt it.'

Bea agreed with him. 'Yes, she was showing off kissing Lewis.'

He shrugged his broad shoulders. 'I still think she's a blether. I doubt there's any truth in what she's making you believe.'

Having got that off his chest, he shrugged as if a weight had lifted.

'Thanks for telling me,' she said.

He nodded firmly

Bea continued. 'Remember the rules. No whirling burls. Keep your kilt pleats neat and your undercarriage private. No high cancan kicks either.'

'Got it.'

'No splits even though technically you wouldn't be showing anything.'

Big Sam winced. 'You're making my eyes water at the thought of it. I've never managed to splay myself, not on purpose, and there could be skelfs on the wooden dance floor. I don't fancy having them plucked out with a pair of tweezers.'

'All the more reason not to do it.'

He nodded, determined to follow the rules.

'Right, let's get you dancing,' she said.

Bea showed him how to place his hands, adjusted his posture and made him stop acting silly.

As they waltzed up and down the living room, she could see him trying his utmost to get it right, and encouraged him. 'You're doing great.'

'I've seen some bridegroom's first dances that are so cringing they'd make your sporran shrink.'

'Well, if you practise, there will be none of that,' she assured him.

They'd decided that three half hour lessons would be sufficient. Bea believed he just needed to calm down a bit, and make sure his first dance with his new bride was something she'd be happy to watch on repeat.

Big Sam stayed a bit longer than his half hour lesson to have a cup of tea and a buttered fruit scone before heading home. He'd learned a lot and intended to practise.

Bea gazed out the bookshop window at the calm twilight, put her jacket on and decided to go for a walk along the shore to get some fresh air.

From the esplanade, she went down on to the sand. The deep blues of the sky arched across the coast and the sea had taken on a twilight glimmer. The light breeze blew through her hair and she walked further than the last time when Lewis had called to her and she'd gone sailing with him. Tonight, she was free to stride as far as she wanted, and she walked a fair distance before heading back along towards the bookshop.

There was still no sign of Lewis' boat.

As she headed up on to the esplanade, Ethel waved to her from her cottage, beckoning to her.

Bea hurried over.

Ethel had just received some news. 'The farmer that Lewis rents his cottage from says that Lewis packed his bags and put everything on his boat before sailing off.'

'So, Lewis isn't coming back?'

Ethel shrugged. 'He's left a few things behind, nothing that someone like him would care about. The farmer told Tavion, and he told me. His lease on the cottage was almost up, but he hasn't tried to renew it.'

'He's gone then.' Bea felt the breeze cut through her.

'I'm sorry, Bea.'

Bea nodded.

'I was finishing my yarn orders before heading over to help Ione,' Ethel explained. 'You're welcome to come with me.'

'I think I'll head back to the bookshop. But thanks.'

Ethel understood.

'Tell Ione that Big Sam did well tonight,' said Bea, before walking away.

'I will. Call if you need me.'

'You too, Ethel.'

Bea walked along to the bookshop, went inside and flicked a cosy lamp on. She'd brought the scent of the sea in with her, and it mingled with her other favourite fragrance — the bookshop. Feeling safe amid the books, she shrugged her jacket off and picked up one of her favourite novels from behind the counter where she'd left it. The book was well read, a copy she'd owned for years, from her personal collection that she'd brought with her from Glasgow.

She curled up in one of the bookshop chairs and began reading it, filling her mind with the story and the characters within it, pushing all thoughts of Lewis away.

The book had fallen from Bea's hand on to her lap when she woke up late at night.

She stretched and stood up, and gazed out at the sea. A storm had whipped up, swirling across the water, causing waves to sweep on to the shore. Somehow she felt it was appropriate, washing away the remnants of Lewis and where his boat used to be, clearing the air.

She hadn't known him long, but some attractions were instant and burned long in the memory. Lewis had made an impression on her, and she supposed it felt all the stronger because she'd started a new life at the bookshop, and it looked like she'd attracted a nice man into her world — unlike the men in her past, someone she could trust and feel secure with. Lewis had fooled her, for whatever reasons, but she still had the bookshop and her friends. She'd build back up from there.

Putting her book safely behind the counter again, she lit the fire in the living room and made tea and toasted tea bread.

By the flickering firelight, she sipped her tea and enjoyed the delicious tea infused loaf rich with mixed fruits.

Then she dug out her knitting needles from her bag and cast on stitches to begin knitting a scarf with Ethel's yarn, using a pattern from Aurora's magazine.

Later that night she snuggled under the covers and fell asleep listening to the sounds of the storm.

The next two weeks flew by in a flurry of increased books sales, sewing bee nights at Ethel's cottage learning how to quilt, improving her embroidery using the floral kit Aurora gave her, making pressed flower books, teaching Big Sam, and enjoying cosy nights in the cottage curled up with a book.

Hilda showed her how to make a small quilt with the fat quarter pieces of fabric and pattern she'd given her.

The photo album in the bookshop now had the pictures from the opening day added.

The excitement was building for the wedding, and the marquee was erected in one of Tavion's fields. The dressmaker wasn't attending the wedding, but she'd contributed to the cost of the reception.

Ione had finished her dress and Bea had seen it during one of the fittings at the sewing bee. It was gorgeous.

Ethel had offered to take Lewis' painting down from the wall of her cottage if it upset Bea. But although Lewis wasn't popular with Bea or the others any longer, they liked his painting. Bea insisted Ethel kept it where it was.

The day of the wedding dawned bright and warm.

Bea put a notice in the bookshop window that she was closed for the day.

The wedding ceremony was being held down on the shore, and floral arches had been set up along with chairs for the guests. Flower petals were scattered to form an aisle for the bride to walk down.

Everyone was seated. Bea wore the tea dress she'd been given by the dressmaker, and styled her hair up at the sides with vintage clasps. Ethel sat beside her, along with the sewing bee ladies. The postmaster sat next to Ethel on the opposite side, continuing to smile and glance at her. Was he hinting that he wished it was them getting married? Ethel seemed happy whatever his thoughts, and the atmosphere was cheerful.

Big Sam stood waiting on Ione. He wore his kilt well. He nodded to Bea and smiled.

Aurora stood at the back filming the event with her phone, and unobtrusively taking pictures. Someone was filming the wedding with a video camera.

The music began to play, and Ione walked down the aisle on the arm of her proud father. There were gasps at the beauty of her fairytale wedding dress. The crystals and sparkles shone in the sunshine, and Ione wore glittering clasps in her hair to complete the look.

'Ione looks beautiful,' Hilda whispered to Bea.

Bea nodded and smiled. She was sure that Big Sam had shed a tear of happiness when he saw Ione walking towards him.

The ceremony itself was lovely, and Bea was delighted for the happy couple.

Far in the distance, Bea saw a boat. For a second, her heart twisted, thinking it was Lewis, but as the boat sailed nearer, she saw it wasn't him.

The moment jarred her, and she shook the feeling aside. Recently, she'd managed to push thoughts of him away most of the time.

Taking a deep breath, she smiled and continued to enjoy the wedding, and followed Ethel and the others as they made their way to the marquee.

The reception in the marquee was filled with music and chatter as people gathered around the floor to watch Ione and Big Sam's first dance. The buffet and toasts had been enjoyed by all, but now it was time for the evening party and dancing. Fairy lights sparkled around the marquee.

Big Sam had changed into his lighter kilt, but Ione still wore her fairytale dress.

The lights were dimmed to highlight the couple, and the music began to play.

Bea was proud of Big Sam's effort to do right by Ione. He stood tall and confident as he held his new bride in his arms, and danced her around the floor. No rules broken tonight.

During the evening, Bea danced with Big Sam, the postmaster, Tavion and several others, including the sewing bee ladies when they did a fast moving circle dance. The energy was incredible. She also danced with Cuan McVey the master chocolatier and Bredon the beemaster. It was the first time she'd met them, and they made her feel welcome. Fintry the flower hunter and his fianceé Mairead had come back from their travels to attend the wedding, and it was wonderful to meet them all.

Late in the night, Bea stepped outside the marquee to breathe in the fresh air, and settle her thoughts. Somehow, she couldn't stop thinking about Lewis. She supposed it was the romance of the wedding. Before going back in, planning to bid goodnight to the happy couple and others, she saw Thimble sitting nearby.

Bea blinked, but the cat was still there, watching her, waiting...

Wishing the new couple well, and hugging Ethel and the others goodnight, Bea headed home to the bookshop. It wasn't far, and she welcomed the relaxing walk in the fresh air to help her unwind from all the excitement.

The breeze blew through her tea dress, and she loved the feel of it.

As she approached the bookshop she blinked twice — Lewis' boat was back — and so was Lewis.

He sat on the harbour wall near his boat and stood up when he saw her.

'Bea,' he called out. 'Can I talk to you?'

His words hung in the clear night air, and for a moment she thought she was dreaming. But as he started to walk towards her, she saw that he was really there.

He wore a classy shirt, open at the neck, and trousers that emphasised his fit build. That handsome face of his was filled with trepidation. No wonder, she thought, prepared to defend herself from whatever tricks he'd planned.

'I don't think we've anything to talk about,' she told him firmly as he closed the distance between them.

Her heart rate increased the closer he came and she almost panicked and ran to the shop to keep herself from him.

'Please, Bea. I know you're upset with me. But at least let me explain.'

If she told him no, she was inclined to believe he'd leave and she'd never see him again. So she nodded curtly, urging him to make it concise, whatever excuses he had.

Other people were beginning to filter down the esplanade on their way home from the wedding reception.

'Can we talk in private in the bookshop?' Lewis asked.

She paused, and then relented. Without a word, she walked towards the shop and unlocked the door.

Lewis followed her and stepped inside.

Bea closed the door and flicked a couple of the lamps on, giving a warm glow to the bookshop.

Taking a deep breath, she faced up to him. 'Okay, I'm listening.'

'First, I'd like to correct the gossip. I'm not involved with Vaila. I've never dated her, and I'm certainly not marrying her in the summer.'

'Vaila painted an entirely different picture,' Bea told him.

'She was lying.'

'Why would she do that?'

'It's complicated.'

'Try me.'

He sighed deeply. 'I didn't want to involve you in any feuds I had with my family. They'd have dragged you into the dispute and used my protective feelings for you against me.'

Bea frowned. 'A dispute with your family?'

'My parents are wealthy, but it's never been enough for them. They own restaurants and a couple of small hotels. My elder brother manages some of them now. His business sense is valuable, and he's ruthless when it comes to business, something I've never liked.'

'I don't understand.'

'I was expected, due to my talent as a chef, to work in the restaurants. My parents have been training me since I was too young to object. I excelled at cooking, but I've never wanted it as a career. I love my art. I've always wanted to paint, and I've made my own success.'

'You're a chef?'

112

'I trained as a chef, and yes, I worked in that field, but not for the love of it.'

'So what happened?' Bea asked.

'Things came to a heated head last summer when I refused to go on any more training courses. They'd booked me on a top patisserie course, and I told them no.'

Bea found herself defending him. 'You've got a right to be your own man, have your own career.'

'They're not the type of people to accept this.' He shook his head. 'I know that some families can have their differences, but I had to break away before I spent another year arguing with them about a future I'm not even getting a chance to enjoy. The dressmaker's letter changed the course of my plans, and I will be for ever grateful to her for that. It made me reconsider my options. Things have felt better living here, working on my paintings, and planning to find a cottage where I can settle down and live my own life.'

'What about Vaila?' said Bea.

'My parents and Vaila's parents are long–time friends. It would've suited them all perfectly if I'd married Vaila and secured the merging of our families. It may seem outdated these days, but that's what it boiled down to. They sent Vaila to entice me, to lure me back to the isle. They used her as a pawn in their selfish game, and she was happy to make the moves they encouraged her to make.'

'This is awful.'

'Can you see now why I didn't want to involve you?'

Bea nodded. 'But I'd have understood.'

'I know, and I love you all the more for it. But heated words said in anger burn deep, causing scars that never fade. I didn't want our life together to start in a blaze of resentment and bitterness.'

'Our life together?'

'Tell me you don't care about me, Bea.'

She couldn't.

'I knew when I first met you that you were the woman for me. I've never felt like that before.'

'You could've told me you were leaving but coming back,' she said.

'No, Vaila had already poisoned things, turning up. I hadn't expected her to do that.'

'I saw her kissing you—'

'I didn't expect her to do that. We don't have that type of relationship. Surely you saw me push her away.'

'No, I didn't. I assumed...'

'That's what she wanted, to cause trouble, and she succeeded.'

'What about the picnic basket, and sailing off with her?'

'The basket was given to me by the farmer's wife when she heard I was leaving the cottage, temporarily. I never cut the lease short. I still have time left in the cottage. I was always coming back.'

She sighed heavily.

'I wanted to settle things with my parents first, and then start afresh here. Hopefully with you.'

'You could've phoned or emailed me.'

'And said what? This is too complicated to explain in a message. I wanted to talk to you in person. I didn't even know when I'd be back.'

'Where did you go?'

'I sailed further up the coast and left my boat there. I didn't want Vaila hanging around causing more trouble for you. I knew she'd leave if my boat was gone.'

'I thought she sailed off with you.'

'No, I sailed off on my own. Vaila drove away in the car she'd hired.'

Bea thought about everything. She hadn't actually seen Vaila sail off with Lewis. He seemed to be telling the truth.

He continued to explain. 'Then I flew to Edinburgh. My agent and my lawyer have offices there. I stayed until I'd legally given up my inheritance and severed all financial ties with my family. The legal side of things took longer than I thought, with my parents blocking my every move. Then my father announced that he was disinheriting me, giving everything to my brother. This settled the issue quicker. So now I'm beholden to no one. I don't want their money, and I certainly don't need it. I haven't taken a penny of it in years, and any that I did receive was hard worked for.'

'You really did work as a chef in their restaurants?' she asked, thinking how efficient he was in her kitchen, and how clean and well kitted out the kitchen was on his boat. It started to make sense.

'I worked as a chef in their restaurants for a few years. Relentless hours. No holidays for the ungrateful son. They put the burden of

114

several restaurants on to me. Finally, I walked away from all of it. We've been at loggerheads ever since.'

'You've made your own success as an artist.'

'Thankfully, and I secured a good agent to make deals for original and limited prints of my paintings. He even sold one of my collections as prints to a hotel and restaurant chain.'

'Oh, dear.' She tried not to laugh.

'Not belonging to my parents,' he said. 'The success of the collection lead to further successes, as my agent sold my work worldwide.'

'Your paintings are beautiful.'

He stepped closer to her. 'But I would've settled for having a little art studio here, making a decent living like others do with their small businesses.'

'Or buy a bookshop?' she teased him.

'I'm glad I was thwarted from all angles on that.'

She looked thoughtful. 'Where do we go from here?'

'I was hoping we could start afresh,' he said, then he seemed guilty.

Bea frowned at him. 'What?'

'I did something before I left Edinburgh. It's impulsive. I probably shouldn't have, but I've never been one to be conventional.'

'What did you do?' She waited to hear that he'd done something dreadful, but instead he reached into his pocket and produced a diamond ring. A dazzling solitaire set in gold. The diamond sparkled under the lights in the bookshop.

She blinked, gazing at it.

'I know it's all the wrong way around, and that we're supposed to date, get to know each other and then I'd give you a ring. But...' he shrugged. 'If you love me half as much as I love you, you'll accept the ring.' He held it out to her. 'Say yes. Let's be happy and make a life together here.'

Her heart pounded and her world changed as she gazed at him. 'Yes, Lewis.'

He put the ring on her finger. 'It'll need adjusted to be the perfect fit. But I think we know a silversmith who'd be happy to do this for us.'

Bea smiled and looked at the ring on her hand. Here she was, wearing the lovely tea dress, and remembering what the dressmaker had said to her. '*Don't let a rival interfere with your happiness. Challenge them. Fight for what you want. You've got it in you to do this.*'

Lewis studied her face. Could he really read her like a book?

'Penny for them,' he said, pulling her close.

Bea smiled at him. 'I was just thinking that we got our happy ending after all.'

Lewis leaned down and kissed her. No books tumbled from the shelves, not tonight. Their story had come to a happy conclusion in the bookshop, where they were about to build a long and loving future together.

End

About the Author:

De-ann Black is a bestselling author, scriptwriter and former newspaper journalist. She has over 70 books published. Romance, crime thrillers, espionage novels, action adventure. And children's books (non-fiction rocket science books and children's fiction). She became an Amazon All-Star author in 2014 and 2015.

She previously worked as a full-time newspaper journalist for several years. She had her own weekly columns in the press. This included being a motoring correspondent where she got to test drive cars every week for the press for three years.

Before being asked to work for the press, De-ann worked in magazine editorial writing everything from fashion features to social news. She was the marketing editor of a glossy magazine. She is also a professional artist and illustrator. Fabric design, dressmaking, sewing, knitting and fashion are part of her work.

Additionally, De-ann has always been interested in fitness, and was a fitness and bodybuilding champion, 100 metre runner and mountaineer. As a former N.A.B.B.A. Miss Scotland, she had a weekly fitness show on the radio that ran for over three years.

De-ann trained in Shukokai karate, boxing, kickboxing, Dayan Qigong and Jiu Jitsu. She is currently based in Scotland.

Her colouring books and embroidery design books are available in paperback. These include Floral Nature Embroidery Designs and Scottish Garden Embroidery Designs.

Find out more at: www.de-annblack.com

Printed in Great Britain
by Amazon

61746980R00071